AF/Inspir
Christiano

JUN 2 8 2004

Copyright © 2001 by Rich Christiano

Published by White Harvest Books, a division of CFG, Inc.
509 Jill Drive, Jonesboro, AR 72404

Printed in the United States of America

LIBRARY OF CONGRESS CATALOGING-IN-PUBLICATION DATA

Christiano, Rich
  Time Changer / Rich Christiano

  ISBN 0-9666911-4-8

  Library of Congress Card Number: 00-111186

For more information about this book, visit our web site:
www.christianmovies.com

THE STORY...BEHIND THIS STORY

The idea for *Time Changer* came in 1989. I have always loved time travel movies and wanted to produce one for the Christian audience, so I started on the screenplay. While working on the first *Time Changer*, I came up with an idea for a second one, too. A sequel.

After taking the next four years to produce two other movies (*The Appointment* and *Second Glance*) I was back working on *Time Changer* in 1993. In fact, I had scouted locations in Memphis, TN and started casting the sixty-minute movie to ready it for production. At that time though, the Christian film industry began going through some major changes. I suspended the filming and turned my attention to the distribution of our movies on video.

Time Changer was shelved.

I spent the next six years primarily developing our distribution until finally producing a new film in 1998 called *End of the Harvest*. All three of the films I made in the 1990's were forty to fifty-five minutes in length and released through Christian distribution channels. Next, I wanted to try producing a feature length Christian movie for theatrical release. There were some new opportunities opening up and the timing seemed right. This would, indeed, be a major project.

Time Changer came front and center again.

I started to re-work the screenplay to see if I could add thirty minutes to make it feature length. I felt the movie had a vital message for our society and I knew if we could produce it for a theatrical release, more people would see the film.

Since I never sent my scripts to other producers, it was not necessary to me for them to be in the correct screenplay format. I did not use the proper headings, scene and character descriptions, scene numbers, etc. As the ninety-minute version of the screenplay started to come together, I started talking with another company about doing a co-production and they wanted to see the script. I knew then that I would have to send them a professional looking script. Along this same time, I was introduced to Greg Mitchell, a twenty-year-old aspiring Christian writer and filmmaker. I read several of Greg's scripts and noted that they were extremely well written. I asked him if he would be interested in re-typing the *Time Changer* script so we could submit it. I also asked Greg to take the time to describe the characters and set the scenes in their proper detail.

When Greg gave back to me the correctly formatted screenplay, the descriptions he added were so good that it gave me the idea to do the novel, which, in turn, I thought would be good promotion for the feature film. I asked Greg if he would be interested in writing a novelization of this screenplay, which he did. Greg took my screenplay and gave it the window dressing it needed to work as a novel. He wrote the draft using my story and dialogue and then I edited the revisions. Thus, the birth of *Time Changer*, the novel, and the story...behind this story.

ACKNOWLEDGMENTS

In most cases, creative endeavors are team efforts. I know it is in filmmaking and this novel was no exception. I want to first thank the talented and gifted Greg Mitchell without whom, there would be no novel. Thanks for taking the project on and giving the story the words it needed. I also owe a great debt of thanks to my friend David Bain who put in many hours editing this manuscript and I used many of his suggestions. Thanks to Judy Anderson who gave me several creative thoughts. I also want to thank Judy's husband, Norris, who has been a fine example to me throughout the years as a mature Christian giving me hours of wisdom and advice pertaining to Christian films. I was excited to use Norris' name as one my key characters in the novel. I want to thank my brother, Dave, who greatly helped me work the story and screenplay back in 1989 and for the title. I want to thank Greg Smith, a good friend of mine, who threw me some solid thoughts. I want to thank John Lawrence, my Pastor and friend who has always supported my projects with honest advice as well as for his story and editorial comments. I want to thank my sister, Robin Ryan, for her story and editing thoughts and her encouragement. Thanks to Bob Heyer for the cover design and his lay-out work. I want to say a special "hello" to all of my relatives, close friends and former classmates who may read this book. I hope you give this story a chance to speak to you.

Finally, I want to thank my wife, Melissa, not only for her story and editing thoughts, as well as the cover photos, but always for her caring love and friendship.

–RC

DEDICATION

I could have dedicated this book to a number of people:
my wife, my parents, family and friends.
But I would rather dedicate it to you, the reader,
in hopes that you will desire in your heart
to be a "time changer".

"Times must change, or time, as we know it...
...will end"

-Russell Carlisle (1890)

CHAPTER ONE

"The Changing Times"

Shafts of light entered through the tall windows and illuminated all but the darkest corners of the staff meeting room. Its centerpiece, a large oak table, with Victorian trimmings was surrounded by six men. These men, Professors and scholars, highly trained and devoted to their areas of expertise, represented the best at Grace Bible Seminary. Here sat the molders and shapers of our future. Eternal future. A heavy responsibility on all of them.

The year was 1890.

The men were discussing quietly among themselves, making small conversation until the large double doors of the meeting room opened. The Dean entered, a well-respected man ready for business, yet with a kind Christian air about him. A hush fell over the room as the professors turned respectively with a smile to their superior. The Dean settled himself behind his tall leather chair and addressed his staff.

"Good day, gentlemen, and thank you for coming. As you know, our Dr. Carlisle has written a new manuscript entitled, '*The Changing Times*'. His publisher wishes a statement from the seminary to put on the back cover of the book which, they feel, shall aid in the book's credibility."

Professor Butler spoke up, "And sales."

The entire room erupted in laughter. The Dean, appreciating the humor, agreed, "Yes, I suppose. Grace Bible Seminary has always maintained the policy all such endorsements be unanimous by our committee, and so now, we shall take this time to express our opinions to Dr. Carlisle."

Dr. Russell Carlisle, a very pleasant looking gentleman in his forties, was known as a man of good intentions, but a bit overconfident in his views. Carlisle nodded his head, welcoming the recognition from his peers.

"You have great courage, Carlisle," Professor Wiseman cautioned with a smile.

Carlisle, always quick with the wit, responded, "Well, if Daniel could face the lions."

Everyone laughed again and Carlisle beamed, delighted his colleagues were in such good humor. This was a big day for him. He had spent months researching this material and had completed three re-writes to get each word exactly so. This book had been tedious work, yet a labor of love. Now, it was finished.

The Dean brought the laughter down again, "For myself, I found it to be highly thought provoking work, Russell, I think it will prove to be a very helpful book to many."

One down, Carlisle thought with a smile, "Thank you, sir."

Turning towards Dr. Gehman, the Dean inquired, "Dr. Gehman?"

Gehman offered his praise with a quick smile, "Good work, Russell, I am proud of you. You have my endorsement."

"Thank you, Kenneth," Carlisle slightly nodded. *Two down.*

"Dr. Wiseman?" the Dean continued.

Wiseman, Carlisle's good friend, couldn't let his endorsement go without a little good-natured ribbing, "Well, despite several misspelled words and much bad grammar, I have no objections."

"Thank you, sir," Carlisle smiled mischievously, "the spelling we can correct. As for the bad grammar, you are criticizing my style."

The room roared in response. After all settled down, the Dean continued with the meeting, "Dr. Henry?"

A very passionate and sober-minded little fellow, Henry was also complimentary, "Insightful, Russell. Excellent reading."

"Very kind of you, sir," Carlisle returned. *What was that? Four now?*

The Dean continued around the table, "Dr. Butler?"

"You have my 'yea' vote, predicated on my receiving a complimentary copy."

Butler topped it off with his mischievous grin. They laughed at his quirky smile.

"We can make those arrangements," Carlisle joked back.

The room laughed again and Carlisle basked in this proud moment. These were the men he admired and respected the most and they were with him. *Excellent,* Carlisle jumped with joy inside, *five down.*

"And Dr. Anderson?" the Dean urged.

Norris Anderson and Russell Carlisle were close

friends and comrades. Norris' father, John Anderson, had been a brilliant scientist, a man of God, and prolific writer for his time. Carlisle was a great admirer and pupil of John's writings. By 1890 though, John Anderson had passed on to be with the Lord, depriving Carlisle the opportunity to actually meet him. Norris, above all others, knew how much this book meant to Carlisle. However, Norris was a man of great conviction. He wouldn't support anything without giving it ample time in thought and prayer. He was not afraid to swim upstream and to stand up for what he believed in, no matter how difficult it might be. Dr. Norris Anderson's approval was singularly the most respected by all there.

So this was it, the moment of truth. The decision to support Carlisle's book had to be unanimous. Carlisle's heart pounded with joy knowing that his good friend Norris was all that stood between Carlisle and his published, endorsed work. Norris hesitated, and with that hesitation, could feel all the attention focusing on him. He began his thoughts with sincere praise.

"Your work shows careful attention to detail, Russell," Norris confirmed, "I can see you did an impressive amount of research."

Wonderful! Carlisle screamed inside. He felt like jumping out of his chair with joy, but contained himself as a proper gentleman did in 1890.

"Thank you, Norris," Carlisle kindly replied.

Assuming this to be an endorsement, the Dean gave Carlisle a small but meaningful smile of congratulations, and was ready to move on to other business.

"Now, I have this statement that I have drafted that can be from the seminary-"

Norris spoke again, cutting off the Dean in respect,

but ready to finish his statement, "However, if I may, Dean, I cannot endorse it in its present condition."

The room was quickly silenced. So much lightheartedness before, now every astonished eye fell on Norris. Carlisle was flabbergasted; his mouth gaped wide open.

The Dean turned towards Norris and gently inquired, "You have a difficulty with something, Norris?"

Norris tried not to make eye contact with Carlisle, knowing he had disappointed his friend. Once they could meet in private, Norris would explain. But not here. Not now. He looked at the Dean and softly replied, "Yes, sir. I do."

The Dean, mildly surprised, but not devastated like Carlisle, nodded in confirmation, and said, "Very well then, I suggest you and Dr. Carlisle discuss this matter privately and we will reconvene at the appropriate time."

Carlisle didn't even hear the Dean. He couldn't believe that Norris, his good friend, had seen fault in his work.

"What do you not agree with, Norris?" Carlisle asked in a disturbed tone.

Norris did not want to argue in public, especially with his friend. He clasped his hands tightly in front of him; aware of the pain he had inflicted. "I would rather discuss this with you privately, Russell."

Carlisle, who was visibly on edge, tried not to explode with rejection, "Let us discuss it now. We have no secrets here."

Dr. Wiseman broke the silence from the rest of the professors, "Yes Norris, I would like to hear your thoughts."

Norris felt the mood in the room change. He understood by criticizing Carlisle's book after each of his colleagues had praised the work, he was criticizing them as well. Norris beckoned to Carlisle again, "I would prefer to discuss this privately."

Carlisle was hurt; his parade was being rained on. This was supposed to be a day of celebration, of rejoicing after months of hard work. He couldn't wait to talk with Norris in private.

"We can discuss it now, " Carlisle declared, "I give you my permission."

Norris was hesitant and with good reason. He knew Carlisle wouldn't listen to him and he wasn't sure how the others would respond. He searched for the kindest words possible, yet, without compromising his beliefs.

"If you wish," Norris said reluctantly. After taking a deep breath, he began his defense. "A major theme in Dr. Carlisle's book suggests that we proclaim and teach the morals taught by Jesus everywhere."

Carlisle protested, "And what is wrong with *that* premise?"

Norris, bracing himself, continued with his statement, "*And*, I am quoting from page twenty-seven, '...even if it is apart from His name and if people are rejecting the authority of Jesus Christ in their lives. We must still teach Christ's ways for the better interest of society. The Lord's ways are best for all.'"

Carlisle, twisting in his chair, interjected, "The Lord's ways *are* best for all."

Wiseman seemed confused. "You cannot be disagreeing with that, Norris."

Norris, holding up his hand, defended, "What Dr. Carlisle is implying is that we can remove the authority of Jesus apart from His teachings, and *this*, I think is deadly."

Dr. Butler, shaking his head slowly, tried to understand, "What do you mean?"

Carlisle, ignoring everyone else in the room, challenged, "You are saying it is wrong to tell a boy not to steal?"

Standing by his convictions, Norris took heart, "Yes, if that is all we say, I think so."

The committee members were again shocked and the room became silent a second time. Norris knew he had become the enemy. He continued, "Without the authority of Christ, mankind is merely left to compare ideas. Morality, then, becomes a matter of opinion. Whereas, one person thinks it is wrong to steal, the next person does not. We need to tell that boy the Lord Jesus Christ says not to steal. Jesus is the authority behind His commands and people need to know and understand that fact. If we remove His authority, we have no basis on which to command. Authority is the issue here."

Carlisle offered an appeal, "Certainly, I agree that it is best but we cannot always mention the name of Jesus because it may not be received, especially by those who have been offended by the church. You are saying that if we cannot mention Jesus we should not advocate His teachings?"

Norris nodded, "Correct."

The Professors shifted in their chairs. There was the sense they were not seeing the depth of Norris' conviction and they were taking him lightly.

"To tell someone not to steal," Norris explained, "without giving them the rightful authority behind the teaching is a moralistic crime."

Wiseman laughed, "A moralistic crime?!"

Butler, smug, retorted, "That is a new term, Norris."

Ignoring those comments, Norris continued, "It is quoting a man without giving credit to the one who said it. When we quote Shakespeare, we say 'Shakespeare says this'. It must be the same with Scripture. Observe the Old Testament as our example. How often do we read where the prophets first say, 'Thus saith the Lord' before they speak?"

Butler, still not understanding, objected, "Yes, but I do not see how promoting the righteous morals taught by Jesus can be wrong."

The others murmured in agreement.

"Gentlemen, please hear me," Norris pleaded, "Satan, our adversary, is not against good morals. He is opposed to Jesus Christ. Thus, Satan is using the teaching of good morals *alone* to deceive people into thinking that they can live a good life to merit heaven."

Carlisle defended himself, "I think we can use morals to attract people to Jesus."

Norris shook his head in disagreement. "Satan is attacking our defenses by convincing us to exclusively teach morals while forsaking the Lord and His gospel. Plus, morals cannot prevent people from sinning before God, only Jesus in the life can do that. Look at our families, they are weakening. One out of sixteen marriages now ends in divorce and our young people are becoming more disrespectful. It is because we are teaching them morals alone and not to submit to the authority of Jesus Christ."

"Norris..." Carlisle's tone was cynical.

Norris rose above the condescending attitudes of his colleagues, "In the case of telling that boy not to steal, if I cannot tell him the command is from Jesus Christ, I would rather say nothing and let him steal. Then, maybe, he will sense his need for the Savior."

"You could not have possibly derived all of this out of that one statement, Norris," Carlisle accused.

"See where the statement leads, Russell?" Norris argued.

Carlisle snapped back, "I think you are taking it down your own path just nicely, *sir.*"

The Dean stepped in. "Gentlemen," he firmly interceded, causing the internal strife to cease for the moment. Norris and Carlisle glared at each other as the rest of the Professors shared a quick glance among themselves. The Dean sentenced the two, as it were, "Now Dr. Carlisle, you and Dr. Anderson will meet privately to discuss your differences, and hopefully each of you will allow the Lord to be your mediator. Later, we shall all reconvene. Until then, let us commit this matter to prayer." The Dean faced the entire group, "Dismissed."

CHAPTER TWO

"A Loophole"

That did not go well, Carlisle thought while sitting at the desk in his empty classroom, his mind still recycling the events from the meeting. This was his book. He had slaved over it and for what? So he could be corrected and rebuked before all of his peers and colleagues? Norris may have meant well, but Carlisle was fighting hard, at this time, just to *like* his good friend.

Carlisle came out of his trance-like state. He began gathering his papers from his desk when Norris stepped through the doorway. Keeping his distance out of respect, Norris didn't feel bad that he stood by his beliefs, but did feel bad that he had hurt his friend's feelings. Almost apologetically, Norris broke the silence, "May I have a word with you?"

Carlisle looked up and after seeing Norris went back to sorting papers, a little more aggressively than necessary. Then, without looking at him, Carlisle answered Norris bitterly, "You have already had quite a few."

Norris sighed, still feeling regret. Inching into the classroom, he moved towards his friend. His stance and demeanor kind and reassuring.

"Now look, Russell, I had wanted to talk privately," Norris reminded him.

"Yes you did," Carlisle agreed.

Carlisle knew what Norris said was true. It was he who had provoked his friend at the meeting. Although Carlisle wasn't ready to admit it, Norris had conducted himself in a Christian manner. Carlisle took his eyes from his papers long enough to present the empty classroom to his estranged friend, "It looks as though you have your wish."

Norris watched his friend's facial expression and knew Carlisle wasn't ready to have a reasonable conversation with him. Taking a bold breath, Norris got down to business, "I want you to come to my house tonight."

Carlisle returned an icy stare to Norris. Then, with a politeness usually reserved for strangers, Carlisle replied, "Thank you, but no, Dr. Anderson."

"I have something I must show you."

"And what would that be?" Carlisle asked, "Your official written criticism of my manuscript?"

"No, nothing like that. Something you must see to believe," Norris patiently replied.

"Can we not take care of it here?" Carlisle insisted, as he returned to sorting and stacking his papers, keeping distant and disinterested. Norris, finding nothing but exhaustion in these games, reached out and placed his hand onto Carlisle's papers, gently pinning them to the desk. He had Carlisle's full attention now. Carlisle looked up at his friend to meet very intense eyes.

"No," Norris began, more forceful than before, "you must come to my house."

With his earlier pain still fueling him, Carlisle was resolute, "And if I shall not?"

Norris stepped back, away from Carlisle, his eyes reflecting a deep sadness. Carlisle stared at Norris. He had seen this look in his friend's eyes before when Norris was deeply troubled and burdened. Maybe, it was time to put his feelings aside. Norris walked to the door and then quickly stopped again.

"Please Russell, come. I have something I *must* show you."

Norris left the room, praying his friend would respond to his plea. Carlisle continued gathering his papers, his hands moving slowly and deliberately as though his mind was not on the task. He began to mentally replay the meeting again in his mind. He looked towards the now empty doorway where Norris had just departed. His disappointment and bitterness quickly returned.

"I shall not," he said to himself.

****

After Norris left, Carlisle sat down at his desk and decided to read some reports that he had planned to take home. Actually, he was hoping one of the other Professors would stop by so they could discuss the situation. No one came and none of the reports he read had the power to hold Carlisle's attention. Frustrated, he gathered his things and walked out of the door.

As he left the hall that housed his classroom and started down the walkway, Carlisle noticed a group of children playing on the lawn under the library windows. The children were pretending to be a church choir, with one young girl taking her place in the front to do the conducting. She was busy waving her arms in the air as the children were singing their rendition of the hymn *"O How I Love Jesus"*. They laughed as they sang, just enjoying some innocent fun.

When Carlisle walked by, his mind was still bothered by the incident with Norris. He stopped and turned on the singing children.

"Will you children be silent?" He growled as he walked towards the tiny choir, "there are students inside studying."

The children immediately looked up at Carlisle, eyes wide and frightened, their song dwindling into silence. They were speechless. Carlisle walked off, not realizing what he had just done. As he marched away, the children quickly scampered in the other direction.

****

Helen was eighteen when Russell Carlisle had met her. Even then, hers was always the voice of reason and sensibility. It was easy to fall in love with her. They had been married for almost twenty years and disagreements were few and far between. Russell never doubted his wife's instinct, her intuition.

Until now.

Pacing the floor, Carlisle mulled over the events of the day in his mind from the committee meeting. How everything was going wonderful, so very wonderful, until Norris interjected his thoughts. What should he do? This book was so important to him. How could he dismiss all of his hard work and research over the complaint of one man, made of flesh and blood, same as he? Then again, how could he dismiss the years of friendship he shared with Norris?

"I do not understand why Norris would want to oppose me," Carlisle confessed to Helen. "This is a good book. All of the other men highly praised the work."

"You should go visit with Norris and talk to him," she kindly offered.

As if not even hearing her, Carlisle replied, "For some reason he is trying to keep the seminary from endorsing my book."

Helen, too, had known Norris for many years and knew he would not respond in such a manner. Not, at least, without good reason.

"Norris is a very wise and kind man. He is not trying to stop the endorsement," Helen said, trying to calm Russell down.

Not convinced, Carlisle quickly responded, "Perhaps Norris is jealous of the work." Carlisle pouted his upper lip, like a small child, his feelings hurt.

Helen stood to her feet and faced her husband, "Dear heart, you know that is not true. Perhaps he has something important to say about it, something you may need to hear." Helen gave her husband a look with a gentle innuendo behind it. Coaxing him. Carlisle was a little agitated by the subtleties of his wife.

"I beg your pardon," he pulled back. *What right does she have to instruct me in this matter? She does not understand what I am going through,* he thought to himself. "I shall not discuss this any further."

Carlisle threw up his hands and walked out of the room. Helen was left behind to watch her husband and could only shake her head in a sigh of disappointment.

****

The clock piece in Norris' hand continued to tick out the minutes and yet, still no sign of Carlisle. *Please, Russell,* his heart called out to the night. He knew Carlisle was angry and the last thing he wanted to do was hurt his friend's feelings. However, the objection he had against the manuscript was not unfounded. He had good reason to be against it, a very good reason, if only his friend would give him the chance to explain. Norris checked the autumn night one last time, hoping that Carlisle had come to his senses and could be seen approaching from afar. Alas, nothing. The night brought no sign of Carlisle.

****

The Dean's office was one of grandeur and beauty with an air of importance that filled its atmosphere. Carlisle often received reassurance for a job well done and gained wisdom from a man he greatly respected in this place.

Today was different.

The Dean could only sit back in his chair and allow Carlisle to get his burden off of his chest.

Already in mid speech, Carlisle continued, "...and truly believe this is my best work. I have poured many months into the research."

"I understand, Russell," The Dean agreed, trying to be sympathetic. "It is a good work. I found it well written."

"The others did as well," Carlisle shouted enthusiastically, then after catching himself, drawing back in afterthought, "if I may say so, humbly. I do not understand Norris. He has always supported me in the past."

The Dean already knew the answer to this next question, for he knew Carlisle well, but he thought it important to get it out in the open, "Have you had a chance to meet with him about the matter?"

Carlisle evaded visual contact with the Dean, "We spoke about a gathering at his home, but...nothing has been set."

The Dean nodded. Carlisle continued with his case, "Sir, I would like to ask if you could make an exception to the unanimous ruling by the board. You saw the reaction of the other men."

The Dean had not expected this. "I cannot change the policy. It must be unanimous. You will have to work out your differences with Dr. Anderson."

Carlisle didn't like the sound of that reasoning, "It seems a shame, though, that because of one, a good work remains unpublished."

The Dean reassured Carlisle, "Your work will get published, but it may not have the seminary's endorsement."

"Yes, however, we both know the endorsement will greatly aid in the work's circulation."

The Dean stood to his feet. He had a meeting in a few minutes and this matter was keeping him from it. Making sure of his sympathy, without alleviating his urgency to leave, the Dean offered, "I am sorry, Russell. I understand your feelings, but there is nothing I can do."

****

Norris was gathering some last minute material before getting ready to leave for his class. He was still sad Carlisle didn't come to visit him last evening. However, he was still hopeful. He knew that this book was too important to Carlisle for the subject to go away. It didn't surprise Norris at all when Carlisle showed up at his office door.

"May we visit for a moment?" Carlisle ventured.

"Yes, I have a few moments before my class."

Norris stood back and waited for Carlisle's apology, or at the very least, an explanation of why he never came to his house last night. However, Carlisle was not there for apologies.

"I am quite surprised that you will not endorse my book," Carlisle began, clearly hurt. "Actually, to be more accurate, I am shocked. You have always supported me in the past."

Norris tried to put his friend at ease, "I told you it was well researched, but…"

Carlisle finished for him, "*But*, telling a boy not to steal is a bad thing if apart from the name of Jesus."

"We must establish a connection between the Lord and His teachings, we must never separate the two," Norris explained. *If only he would put his stubbornness aside and come to my house.* "I have invited you to my house to explain why I am saying this." As he said that, Norris remembered Carlisle's absence the night before, "I was disappointed not to see you last evening."

Disregarding his friend's feelings, Carlisle continued in his discussion of the manuscript, "The others, including the Dean, have all endorsed it. Do you see yourself as better than these fine men?"

"Oh, come now, Russell. Why do you say such a thing?"

"Why does it have to be at your home? Let us discuss the matter here and now."

"This is not the place nor is now the time."

Norris stood to his feet and prepared to leave for his class. Then, with one last thought, and urgency in his eyes, Norris turned to Carlisle. "You must come to my house."

The pleading in Norris' eyes spoke eloquently. He *knew* something. If only Carlisle would receive it.

"I do not understand your stand against the book," Carlisle continued, taking a deep breath, lashing out, "I am suspecting jealousy."

Shaking his head, Norris went out the door, calling out behind him, "I hope to see you this evening. Then my friend, you will understand."

****

Helen was working hard on a floral arrangement at the Carlisle home. She was pruning some flower buds and polishing some leaves while holding them delicately as if these wonderful creations of God were newborn babes. There was a knock on the door. Confused, not expecting any visitors at this hour of the day, Helen made her way to the front door and opened it. A lanky messenger boy greeted her.

"Telegram for Dr. Russell Carlisle."

He handed her a telegram and tipped his hat in greeting. She took the telegram from his hand with a smile and watched in curious humor as he rushed away before she could even thank him.

****

As Helen received the strange telegram, Carlisle was a few blocks away at Grace Bible Seminary tutoring one of his young charges in the courtyard. He appeared to be in deep explanation when Dr. Wiseman noticed him from afar. Seeing his colleague, Wiseman journeyed over to Carlisle's circle.

After seemingly explaining the complex matter to the young man, Carlisle sent him away with a hearty and reassuring pat on the back. Wiseman approached, just then, with his greetings, "How is the author doing?"

Carlisle considered for a moment, then replied, sullenly, "I would be doing very well if Dr. Anderson would endorse my book."

"You two still having a bit of a difference?" Wiseman raised an eyebrow, already suspecting discourse between the two friends.

"He is holding out for some reason," Carlisle leaned in closer, as if discussing some secret, "I am starting to think he is jealous of the writing."

Wiseman tried to stifle a laugh at his, sometimes, over-dramatic colleague, "I see."

Carlisle continued, "I even spoke with the Dean about making an exception to the unanimous policy this one time."

"And?"

"He said the endorsement must be unanimous. It is seminary policy."

Carlisle seemed defeated, but Wiseman's mind was at work, "You could get the policy changed."

Carlisle's eyes glimmered, "What do you mean?"

"A seventy-five percent majority vote by the seminary board of directors can overrule any seminary policy in place."

That is it! Carlisle's soul jumped for joy. However, he maintained his stuffy dignified air. "Are you sure?" He asked in confirmation.

"Quite sure," Wiseman nodded.

Carlisle's mind began to race at all of the possibilities, "Yes, if we can change the unanimous ruling policy, I could receive the seminary's endorsement."

Wiseman slowed his friend down. "I am only pointing out a possibility."

However, despite Wiseman's interjection, Carlisle wasn't listening. He was now caught in a uneasy, ethical entanglement, "Oh, but could I do that to Norris? We are good friends. He may not speak to me again should I try this."

Wiseman interceded again, explaining his motives. "It was never my intention to break up your friendship with Dr. Anderson."

Carlisle stopped pondering his debacle to listen to his friend's advice.

"However," Wiseman continued, "I too, in times past, have questioned the unanimous policy in my mind. It seems to me we are not going to see eye to eye on every last detail in our published works."

Carlisle listened carefully, taking mental notes. He must meet with the Dean.

****

The Dean was, once again, leaning back in his office chair, trying to be polite as he listened to Carlisle's persistent objections. Fresh off of his talk with Wiseman, Carlisle was already putting Wiseman's thoughts to his use.

"It seems to me we are not going to see eye to eye on every last detail in our published works. Personally, I cannot see why Dr. Anderson's disagreement should stand in the way of the seminary's endorsement." Carlisle took a breath and then reassured his feelings of Norris to the Dean, "No offense taken towards our good friend."

The Dean breathed deep and prepared himself like a father might do in the face of two bickering sons, "Is there not any way you can work this matter out with Dr. Anderson before taking this next step?"

"I have tried to reason with Dr. Anderson and will continue to do so. However, I have worked very hard on this publication and it is very disheartening to publish a work without the endorsement of this seminary."

The Dean thought it over and regretfully addressed Carlisle's request, "I will file your request tomorrow and try to set up a meeting early next week."

Carlisle nodded in over eager appreciation. His smile wasn't hidden easily.

The Dean appealed, "However, do try to speak with Dr. Anderson about this matter one last time to see if you can resolve your differences."

Carlisle readily agreed, "Thank you sir, and I will try to speak with Dr. Anderson."

CHAPTER THREE

"No One Must Know"

Carlisle stared down at his telegram; the very one Helen received earlier in the day. In fact, he had been staring at it so long that his evening cup of tea had grown cold, while Helen still sipped on hers.

She saw the grim set in his eyes and spoke softly, "You seem unhappy."

No response.

"I believe the board will change the policy and you will receive your endorsement," she smiled, trying to reassure her husband.

Carlisle wasn't so convinced, "Yes, but we may be too late."

He turned back to the telegram and read the words again. It was a notice from the publisher. His deadline for publication was growing close and Carlisle had to make a decision. He relayed his dilemma to his beloved, "The publisher wants to take the book to press next week. There is some urgency to get the work out, some distribution opportunities that they do not want to miss. I may not be able to get the meeting assembled in time to get the endorsement I desire."

Carlisle thought about this latest development. Then, he began to seriously consider what he was doing and what it could mean to Norris. In a much quieter, more serious tone, he poured out his heart, "I fear this incident might seriously breach my friendship with Norris."

As that thought started to sink in, Carlisle felt a little guilty. Helen began to see the warmer side of Russell, the side she fell in love with so long ago. She got up from her seat and crossed the distance to him. Placing a sympathetic hand on his shoulder, she comforted him, "Go visit Norris. He is a reasonable man. I am sure you two can work this matter out."

Carlisle looked to her and smiled. They shared a quiet moment and Carlisle realized what he should do. Now, the only hard part was actually doing it. As if sensing his doubts, Helen smiled and raised an eyebrow, "Besides, you promised the Dean."

****

It was a beautiful night, wonderful weather for a walk. However, Russell Carlisle was blind to the evening's beauty as he strode quickly in the brisk air. Carlisle arrived at Norris' home, one of great splendor. Russell and Helen had enjoyed many visits there, but Carlisle was not here for a cup of tea this time. He was on a mission. Get in, get out. He marched up the steps to the front door, only to have the front door open before him. A very pleased and excited Norris stepped out, "I am so glad you came, Russell."

Carlisle, still distant and a bit perturbed, rambled, "My publisher needs to go to printing, so we must settle our misunderstanding."

Norris, very excited that his guest had come over, knew Carlisle had no idea what was the true purpose for tonight's visit. He gestured towards the backyard, "Follow me."

Although the house was elegant notwithstanding, Norris' backyard was something entirely different. Out here, surrounded by indifferent trees, a large barn house rested out of sight. It was old, ancient in comparison to the house, a relic from the past. Something that stood here long before Norris' stately dwelling. Definitely not something one would expect to hold any kind of mystery. As Norris led Carlisle to the barn house, he began rummaging through a giant ring of old keys, trying to find the right one. He was trying to contain his excitement, too. Carlisle was just along for the ride.

"What I am about to tell you, as well as show you," Norris began as he found the appropriate key, "must be sworn to total secrecy. Do I have your word?"

Carlisle, not seeing the reason for all of this drama, made his response short, "Yes, what is it?"

Norris wasn't quite convinced, "No one must know."

Raising a suspicious eyebrow, Carlisle nodded, "Yes, of course."

With a sigh of relief and anticipation, Norris pushed the doors wide open and the two entered. The entire barn seemed to be packed with equipment. Wires, levers, gauges, pistons, and parts of all shapes and sizes lined their path as the two of them moved forward. Carlisle's head was spinning back and forth amazed at what he saw.

As he strained to get a better view of some of the

devices, the two continued to move towards a particular corner of the barn.

Norris explained, "I am sorry you never met my father, Russell. He loved the Lord and was a godly man."

Carlisle, still gawking at this equipment, replied, distracted, "I am sorry, too. I have enjoyed reading the writings of John Anderson. His articles on science and the Bible are brilliant works."

"My father was fascinated with inventing," Norris added, "it was his hobby."

"An inventor. I did not know."

"Yes. In fact, it seems I may have inherited his passion myself."

Carlisle looked at his friend in surprise, "You, too? I had no idea."

"Shortly before my father went to be with the Lord, he came up with something, a theory, something incredible. He completed his project, yet sadly died before he had the opportunity to test it."

Ogling over a small device with wires and gauges covering it, Carlisle urged his friend, "Go on."

Norris had now positioned Carlisle in a corner of the barn right in front of a grated metal platform. Above the platform, one could see the brilliant night, as there was a hole cut in the barn roof. The moonlight cast its glow over the two men. An extremely large panel board filled with knobs and levers sat to the left of the platform and a sizable circular pipe connected the two.

Norris revealed this latest discovery. "My father invented *this*."

The building suspense and climax of revelation didn't quite explain everything to Carlisle who looked perplexed, "What is it?"

Norris wasn't able to resist a mysterious reply, "Something incredible."

Norris Anderson was thrilled. This had been a family secret he had kept for too long, always itching to reveal it to someone. And now, for reasons Norris was beginning to understand, Russell Carlisle was that someone.

Carlisle turned to his friend, wanting more answers, "But, what is it?"

Norris was still trying to build the anticipation, "It's a quantum chrono displacement device."

A moment passed and Carlisle realized that he still didn't know anything, "A what?"

"My father's technical term," Norris clarified. "It is a transporter of sorts. Russell, this machine can transport a man...through time."

Carlisle exploded with laughter. Norris' mystique was sort of deflated as he stared at his friend. Still chuckling, Carlisle managed, "That is impossible."

"The Lord has allowed it," Norris pleaded, "He gave my father the wisdom to create all of this. My only regret is that my father was never allowed to experience time travel himself."

"Then how do you know it works?" Carlisle challenged as he tried to contain his laughter.

"I tested it," Norris assured confidently.

"*You* tested it?!"

Norris smiled, feeling the upper hand in the adventure category, "Yes I did."

Carlisle still did not believe, "You have traveled through time?!"

"Yes. I went over one hundred years into the future."

"Over one hundred years?" Carlisle did the quick math in his head. "To the twenty-first century?!"

"Correct," Norris confirmed.

Carlisle couldn't grasp all of this. In fact, he down right refused to grasp any of it.

"No, that is not possible," Carlisle grumbled.

Norris continued to plead and convince his friend, "It is the truth, Russell."

"What proof do you have?" Carlisle demanded.

Norris was a bit hesitant knowing that his answer would damage his case.

"I have tried to acquire some physical evidence but the machine will not allow us to pull anything back from the future."

Now, Carlisle thought he had the upper hand. "And why not?"

"Because that article would not yet exist. It would be impossible for me to show you a coin from the 1950's before it was minted."

Norris' answer was a logical one. How could one bring something back from the future before it was created? Carlisle, though, too amused with the premise to take this answer seriously, answered sarcastically again, "Oh, I see."

Carlisle still believed he had Norris in a deep hole on this one. The absurdity of traveling through time. Perhaps this revelation could help Carlisle build a case against Norris for not supporting the book by saying he had gone crazy. On the other hand, Norris knew well that "seeing was believing". He started digging out of his hole.

"I did not expect you to believe me, Russell. So I have taken the liberty to arrange a journey for you."

"A journey...where?"

"Into the future."

"Oh, come now."

"I want you to see where the teaching of good morals *alone* leads to, Russell. I want you to see for yourself what happens when we take the authority of Jesus out of our lives."

Carlisle took hold of Norris' coat collar, trying to coax some reason into him. He formed his words very slowly, as if explaining a complex matter to a child. "It is impossible to travel through time."

Norris didn't slow down. "There will be no need for you to worry about Helen or your classes. When you leave tomorrow night, you will return from the future only seconds after you had originally left."

Fed up, Carlisle refused to listen, "I shall not listen to anymore of these delusions."

He let go of Norris and marched out of the barn towards the house. Norris stopped to hurriedly lock the padlocks to the shed. Then, he rushed to catch up. Carlisle was now making comments aloud to himself about the absurdity of what he had just heard. Norris called out as he finally caught up to his distraught friend, "Russell, please."

Carlisle was of no mind to listen, "I am leaving."

Norris made one last convincing attempt, "You must see for yourself what happens in the future."

No reply came from Carlisle. Feeling defeated, Norris stood there and watched Carlisle walk away, until he disappeared into the night.

"You must," he said softly to himself.

CHAPTER FOUR

"Tomorrow Night"

It was early afternoon and the sun was making its daily pilgrimage across the brick structure, which housed Grace Bible Seminary. This institution had served as a light to the world for many years preparing young men for the ministry of the Lord. Russell Carlisle loved it there. In fact, this was his fourteenth year as a professor. Nothing gave him greater satisfaction than helping prepare young men to teach God's Word, pastor churches and to preach the gospel. The students respected him as an elder and a passionate, scholarly mentor. Carlisle himself once thought about serving the Lord in the ministry as a pastor, but because of youth and inexperience, he feared his inability to speak in front of large crowds. He had always felt the need, though, to expound truth, and realized published books could become his voice. It would be his way to communicate his thoughts and opinions to a world in need of hope.

Although Carlisle loved teaching each and every day, today was difficult. His mind was divided while he taught his classes. His encounter with Norris the night before and all this nonsense about "time travel" bore on his mind. He was finding it harder and harder to concentrate, wishing more to sit down and settle this dispute with Norris once and for all, as well as putting an end to the time travel talk. The phrase "tomorrow night" kept ringing in Carlisle's mind. Tomorrow night, now tonight, they would attempt the impossible.

Time travel.

The thought made Carlisle nervous. *Has Norris gone mad?* Carlisle thought to himself. However, in reality, Carlisle knew better. Norris had always been known as a very credible, honest man; always straightforward and motivated by his convictions. Maybe, that's why the time travel talk was troubling Carlisle so much and making him so anxious. Norris never lied, at least, based on the things that Carlisle knew of him.

Pondering over this, Carlisle was bringing his final teaching session for the day to a close. He turned to his students, who eagerly listened to his words, "And remember, Science and scientific findings do not make the statements in the Bible true. The Scriptures are always true and never need verification. Scientific support of the Scripture only proves the science to be true, not the Scripture. My advice to any scientist is to make sure his findings coincide with God's Word," he paused, preparing that wit, "If, of course, he wants to be a good one."

The young men all laughed as the school bell rang. Politely and quietly, they began gathering their things as Carlisle finished, "Tomorrow we shall speak on Jesus' view of the Scriptures out of Matthew, chapter four."

The students began making their way for the exit, greeting Dr. Anderson who had nudged his way through the door into the classroom. Carlisle's stance revealed his unhappiness in seeing his friend. Norris, though, was confident about the coming events of this evening. He waited for the room to completely empty before he approached Carlisle, with excitement in his voice.

"Everything is set for tonight. You depart at eight o'clock."

Carlisle instantly became edgy. "Everything is set for what?"

Norris inched in closer, his eyes wide with wonder and mystery, "For your journey."

Carlisle, fed up with this nonsense, snapped back, "Oh, come now, Norris. I stayed awake half the night thinking about this absurdity. I am beginning to think that you are on the verge of lunacy."

Norris was offended. "You still do not believe me?"

"Do you really expect me to?"

"I expect you to explore the possibility," Norris reasoned.

"What possibility? It is impossible to travel-" then after realizing how loud he'd become, Carlisle lowered his voice so as not to draw attention, "- travel through time and I will not be made a part of any jest."

Norris defended his position again, "Russell, we cannot continue our disagreement forever and your journey will resolve our differences."

"I simply do not know why you are doing this," Carlisle said as he tried to make Norris feel foolish about the idea.

"Please come to my house tonight at eight o'clock," Norris pleaded again.

This was too much for Carlisle, a challenge greater than his understanding. He ignored Norris and began gathering his papers. Norris turned and headed for the door. Carlisle, still not looking at Norris, declared his position. "I am not coming."

"You must," Norris answered, now at the doorway. He then paused for a moment, looking both ways down the hall making sure no one was able to hear his reply as he finished, "Eight o'clock."

Carlisle pretended not to hear him. Finally, he glanced towards the door but Norris was gone.

****

The sun was down. The autumn wind had picked back up but it was a marvelous evening. Carlisle saw it as a perfect opportunity to sit at home, with all of his windows open, and enjoy a nice book. Nothing could go wrong on a night like this.

Carlisle rested in his plush velvet chair laying his head on the back of the chair. He closed his eyes, just for a moment, and absorbed the atmosphere. The wind peacefully invaded his home and danced with the drapery on the window. His nerves were finally settled. He had thought long and hard about this "time travel" nonsense and decided it was all a waste of his time. He would not go to Norris' house tonight. When his friend asked him in the morning about his absence, Carlisle would settle this fairy tale once and for all.

With a smug grin of superiority, Carlisle lifted his book back to his eyes and began reading again. *No, this time travel business does not even deserve a second thought.* He went back to reading. Then, he noticed his grandfather clock staring back at him from across the room. The time read seven fifty-eight. Carlisle noticed the time. He went back to reading but realized that he'd read the same sentence three times now. He wasn't getting anywhere.

Seven fifty-nine.

He couldn't keep his eyes off the time. It haunted him. No, worse, taunted him. He could feel butterflies taking up flight in his stomach. He was utterly transfixed by the second hand, watching time literally slip away. He tried to shake it all off, pretending not to care. Oh, but he did care. He looked at the clock again.

Eight o'clock.

The old grandfather clock, with aged wisdom, began to chime. ONE. Carlisle tried to read.   TWO. It was impossible to read. THREE. *No. This is inconceivable.* FOUR. *I am not going over there.* FIVE. *Norris will just have to wait until morning.* SIX. *Yes, morning.* SEVEN. *And the sooner I go to sleep...* EIGHT. *The sooner I will end this nonsense.*

Carlisle slammed his book closed and jumped up out of his chair. "Oh bother."

Grabbing his Bible, Russell Carlisle headed for the door.

****

Norris could hardly contain his excitement as he and Carlisle moved towards the time machine. Carlisle, with Bible in hand, was there for an entirely different reason, ready to settle this dispute once and for all. Norris, though, was caught up in a whirlwind of activity as he moved everything to position, throwing switches, powering up, and connecting wires. He began giving Carlisle important instructions as he prepared the machine.

"I have arranged your journey," Norris said as he turned a bright red knob, "so that you will be arriving on a Saturday at noon and returning the following Wednesday evening at nine PM. This will give you over four days in the future. Your entry point will be a secluded alley in the city where I made my first entry. Make sure you are back at this same point at nine PM on Wednesday for your return. Theoretically, you should come back from the future no matter where you are, but by being at your point of entry, we can be assured of your safe return."

As Norris stopped to plug three connecting wires, Carlisle saw this as an opportunity to make his case, "Norris, I came here to reason—"

Norris didn't allow Carlisle to finish his sentence. Instead, he pointed over to a clock face, stripped of its foundation and base. Its sole decoration was fifty or more wires dangling from behind its brain.

"This is a timer," Norris displayed. "When your time reaches nine o'clock on Wednesday night, it will activate the transporter automatically and you will be pulled back. This is how I traveled alone."

Carlisle was still trying to be polite, "Norris, this is impossible. Can we please just sit down as two mature Christian men to discuss this matter?"

Norris was too caught up in his activities to answer Carlisle's question but continued delivering his own important instructions, "I would not tell anyone you are from the past. It will only cause you difficulties."

Carlisle was beginning to lose his patience.

Norris continued, "And do not try to look up your own fate, for it will not be revealed to you."

Carlisle spoke boldly. "I demand that this nonsense stop right now so we may settle our differences!"

Norris stopped to eye his friend for a moment, "Russell, your journey into the future will settle our differences." Seeing that as the end of that, Norris reached into his pocket and retrieved a small leather pouch handing it to Carlisle. "Here, take these."

Carlisle untied the pouch and spilled some of its contents into his other hand. Norris had given him several coins. "What are these for?" Carlisle asked.

Norris explained, "You will need money for food and clothing in the future, and to find an inn to stay at. You can exchange these for modern currency when you arrive. Just visit a store called 'The Coin Exchange.' It is located on Main Street. They will help you." Then as a side note, "You simply will not believe the price of merchandise. Lucky for you, these coins are worth a lot of money where you are going."

"Oh, come now, Norris," complained Carlisle, still disbelieving.

Laying an encouraging hand on Carlisle's shoulder, Norris interrupted, "This is a divine opportunity for you. You must see, with your own eyes, where the teaching of morals *alone* will lead." And with that encouraging hand, Norris pushed Carlisle over to the platform into a chamber that was directly under the hole in the roof. "Now please, stand here."

Carlisle had tried to be kind but was just about fed up and protested again, "This jest has gone far enough."

The machine started to make a little noise. Norris continued, marveling at his father's creation, "It is fantastic, is it not? This machine works by stored rays and energy from the sun. Bottled up and time-released, it acts as a transporter, displacing you through time at incredible speeds with great accuracy."

The night sky and chilly breeze poured in from the hole in the barn roof. Norris pointed to it, explaining, "The hole is here to assure us of no interference with the process. When the machine is fully activated, it creates cosmic strings, of sorts. Like a wire tapping into the vastness of space and time. Think of this as a small creek running off into a larger time stream." Norris winked, impressed with his own useful analogy, "It is much more complicated, but we do not have the time to discuss such matters."

Norris turned his gaze from the gaping hole above him and looked to his friend with a smile as the noise increased, "You have an important journey to make."

Carlisle protested for the final time, "Norris, this silliness has gone on for long enough."

Norris smiled, disregarding the complaints. He returned to his work, still talking with his friend, "I wish I could come with you, Russell, but I have yet to calculate a way to transport two travelers simultaneously. Rest assured, I will keep trying."

Preparing for final activation, Norris approached the main lever. He looked around at the laboratory. This was it. The culmination of his father's work now rested with him. The moment where dreams and fantasies become an incredible pursuit to change the world for the better. A way to make a difference in the human stream. He was very proud of this moment. Up until now, time traveling exploits were for experimentation. Now, some good might finally come of this. The noise from the machine grew much louder.

"I am about to leave," Carlisle said, making his last stand and final attempt to reason.

Norris turned to him with a sly smile and yelled over the noise, "Yes my friend, you *are*."

As the noise increased, and Norris' countenance appeared deadly serious attending to his activities, Carlisle began to get worried. He took notice of the chamber that Norris had placed him in, clinging only to his Bible and the pouch of coins.

Norris was by the main lever, waiting for the right moment as the machine's noise increased. Then, as the deafening roar threatened to shatter the night air itself, the moment came, "Russell...observe."

Norris threw his full weight into the main lever. Steam escaped in violent hissing from various portions of the huge machine. Slowly at first, then evolving into a rapid motion, the pistons and gears began to beat a rickety rhythm. The whole barn came to life. Shaking, rattling, breathing, coughing out the dust that had settled since its last use. The machine roared with energy. It surged with life.

Norris shouted to Carlisle one more piece of instruction, "Look up a man by the name of Mitchell Bain. You will find him at the public library. He knows me but not where I am from. He will be helpful to you."

Norris grabbed a pair of goggles from the workbench and strapped them on, preparing for what he knew came next. Two rings of steel around Carlisle's chamber now began to turn, one clockwise and the other counterclockwise.

"Remember," Norris screamed, over the deafening roar, "Wednesday night! Nine o'clock! The entry point!!"

A brilliant ray of luminous light emitted from the machine into the chamber and totally surrounded Carlisle so that he could not be seen. As the light and the noise intensified to an incredible pitch, Norris barely heard Carlisle's voice yell from inside the chamber, "Norris, what is happening?"

The contained light and energy rays could no longer be contained as both exploded outwards from the edges of the chamber off the platform rocketing towards the heavens. The cosmic strings. The ray of light stretched all the way into the stars of the night until it disappeared from the human eye.

Carlisle, with his Bible and the pouch of coins, suddenly vanished...

CHAPTER FIVE

"When Am I?"

Russell Carlisle was left standing there, eyes closed, not completely sure what had just transpired. "Norris?" he said softly. No answer. Carlisle could hear undefined noises in the far background, but they seemed muffled as if from a tunnel. "Norris," he said in a loud whisper, eyes still closed. "Are you there?" Still no reply. Finally, he summoned the courage to open his eyes. It was almost too much to bear. *It appears to be an alley,* he thought to himself. *What...where...this cannot be...But, this looks like an alley and Norris said...no, it just cannot be, I shall not believe it.* Then, Carlisle noticed the Bible that he clutched for dear life still in his hand and the small pouch of coins in his pocket that Norris had given him. It was starting to set in. *Had it really happened? Could I actually be in the future?* Bright daylight at the mouth of the alley began calling to him. He knew he had to look. To make sure, once and for all. Carlisle proceeded forward, staying near the alley wall to protect him, as he emerged from the dark alley. And what he saw...

NOISY TRAFFIC. HORNS HONKING. TALL BUILDINGS. SHINY CARS. BLARING STEREOS. MODERN CIVILIZATION. NOT *CARLISLE'S* CIVILIZATION. OCEANS OF PEOPLE IN STRANGE CLOTHING. ADVANCED TECHNOLOGY. THE STREET LIGHTS. STOP. GO. WALK. DON'T WALK. TOTAL CONFUSION...THE PRESENT...was too much for him!!

The images and the confusion overwhelmed Carlisle and drove him back into the alley, almost hyperventilating. Panic! He held his hand over his mouth to muffle a scream. Shaking! He wanted to go home. *This cannot be real. Time travel is not real. This is a dream, no a nightmare!*

While backing into the alley trying to forget what his eyes had seen, Carlisle noticed a discarded newspaper lying on the ground. He stared at it for a moment, its pages beckoning him to read. Proof. He started for the paper, picked it up, but was afraid to look at the date. This date would seal his destiny. Prove time travel was possible. He didn't want to, but he had to. Had to look at it. He unfolded the pages and read the date. His eyes bulged, "Two-thousand and——".

Just then, a delivery truck sped by scaring Carlisle half to death. He dropped the paper and backed against the wall trying to catch his breath in total disbelief. He looked at the paper again, a distance off, on the ground. The date, though barely legible, acted as if it was staring back at Carlisle. "I do not believe it." Carlisle whispered in complete amazement. "I *am* in the future."

****

Carlisle clumsily made his way down the busy streets, taking everything in. Nobody paid attention to him. True, he was wearing his 1890 apparel, but in this time, that was tame. Carlisle didn't notice either. He was fascinated. Everything was so...big. Big. Shiny. New. He had to keep himself from running into a few innocent bystanders. Russell Carlisle, a man of order, was not paying attention to where he was going. He was gawking, staring at the skyline. The buildings seemed to reach all the way to the heavens. What started out as frightening now seemed exciting. Carlisle couldn't wait to see how the people of this time had used all of these marvelous advances to further the Lord's work. He was certain this would prove to be a most wonderful era in human history.

****

His first order of business was to locate "The Coin Exchange" on Main Street, which Norris had told him about so he could exchange his coins for properly dated currency. The place wasn't very busy, just a few people here and there. Carlisle made a special point to smile and offer a "good day" to everyone he made eye contact with. All he got in return were strange looks, as other patrons continued with their business. Of course, his 1890 apparel didn't help.

A worker had just finished with his customer as Carlisle stepped up to the counter. The man smiled, at first, as was the job requirement. His smile quickly faded as the image of Carlisle fully registered, then he gave him a quizzical look. The worker, a man in his fifties, tried not to stumble. "Can I...help you?"

Carlisle stretched a grin across his face like a small

child. *Someone from the future talked to me!* He quickly and obediently pulled out his pouch and emptied its contents on the counter. The coins spilled out.

"Sir, I need to exchange these for more appropriate currency," Carlisle said, excited to make his first transaction with a future man.

The worker was visibly taken aback by the coins, "Where did you get these old coins?"

Carlisle felt a slight case of panic come over him. Thinking fast he said, "A...friend of mine...left them for me."

Picking a couple up and studying them in awe, the worker replied, "They're beauties."

Carlisle smiled, a bit on edge, not knowing what to expect. "Yes...they are," he said, trying not to draw attention.

"They almost look new," the worker replied turning to a co-worker nearby showing him the prized spoil. A commotion began as two or three more people huddled around the old coins. Carlisle became more and more uncomfortable. *Did I do something wrong?* Carlisle wondered. Finally, after what seemed an eternity to Carlisle but was really only about five minutes, the worker returned and scrawled a figure on a slip of paper showing it to Carlisle.

"I can only give you this much for them, Mr.-"

"Carlisle," he volunteered.

"Mr. Carlisle," the worker finished, "Is this amount acceptable?"

Carlisle paused for a moment, smiled, and replied politely, "Whatever you decide, good sir. I only expect to be treated in a Christian manner."

The man gave Carlisle a strange look and a nearby secretary stopped typing for a moment on her computer.

When Am I?

Did I do something wrong again? Carlisle wondered to himself. The worker had been caught off guard.

****

The Excelsior Hotel was beyond anything Carlisle could ever imagine. It towered over all the other buildings on its block and absorbed the radiant sun. Constructed only a year ago, this hotel stood as the pinnacle of technological advancement in the field of accommodations. Carlisle wanted to experience the best that the future had to offer. He was also decidedly against spending his short time here in some filthy desolate locale.

Bellhops were earning their keep as Carlisle watched the amazing hotel lobby at work. A huge fountain greeted all the visitors and Carlisle could not help but stare in awe. Finally, he managed to proceed to the registration desk and obtain a room. A bellhop came to assist him, even though Carlisle came to the future with a Bible as his sole piece of luggage.

****

The door to Carlisle's hotel room swung wide open and Carlisle slowly peered in. Escorting him on his tour was his bellhop. The room housed everything one could want in a hotel room. A King size bed. A great view of the bustling city. A full size bathroom, complete with a Jacuzzi. A grand entertainment system. To say the least, Carlisle was impressed. Nothing impressed the bellhop, he'd seen it all before, about twenty times a day to be exact. The bellhop, having more important places to be, hurriedly showcased this luxurious room.

"I trust that you will find your accommodations acceptable," he said urgently, ready to move on to his next customer.

Carlisle, not quite catching on to the bellhop's hurry, could only whisper his approval in surprise, "Oh my, this is quite exquisite."

"Yeah, it's great, isn't it?" The bellhop agreed sarcastically. He quickly moved along in the tour, showing Carlisle the finer things.

"Keep in mind our televisions now feature satellite hook ups with over one hundred and fifty channels for your viewing enjoyment."

Without giving Carlisle a moment to register any of what was said, the bellhop moved to the cabinet and opened it, revealing the entertainment center and at its center, a big screen television. He took the remote and handed it to a rather confused Carlisle, who was still trying to catch up to the train of thought.

"Television?"

"Plus," the bellhop continued, "you can also receive over one hundred radio stations through the TV. Digital, of course."

"Digital?"

"If you need to go online, we have a separate computer line next to the phone."

"Online?"

The bellhop suddenly noticed that Carlisle was repeating everything he said. He stopped in his monologue and turned to Carlisle, "You okay, sir?"

Carlisle caught his mouth hanging open and quickly closed it, not wanting to draw more attention to himself, "I am sure I will find my way around. Thank you."

The bellhop nodded, barely accepting that, while

moving for the door. Carlisle followed. The bellhop waited for his customary tip. Carlisle reached out and shook his hand saying, "Thank you for your help my good man, and may the Lord bless you."

The bellhop looked at his hand and then Carlisle in a strange way as if wondering which planet this guy was from. He spoke again, a bit mockingly, "You must have come in on a long flight, still suffering from jet lag, eh?" The bellhop tipped his hat grumbling to himself on his way out.

Carlisle was left in another world trying to under-stand, "Jet lag?"

CHAPTER SIX

"The Adventure Begins"

After setting his Bible on the table, Carlisle quickly left the hotel not wanting to waste a single moment of this trip. There was so much to see and do, a whole new world to explore. So far however, Carlisle hadn't seen anything that suggested that his theory on morals was harmful. Everyone, though somewhat strange, seemed pleasant enough. Perhaps, Norris was just overreacting. His convictions were always a little stronger than Carlisle's. Yes, that was it; Norris was just being Norris. *Things are fine here*, Carlisle reasoned.

As Carlisle joined the herd of people on the streets, he observed businessmen and women marching, seemingly, in a stupor along their way. They were all stone faced and busy with their determination for success or survival propelling them, single mindedly, to their next stop. Carlisle though, had no such determination. He wandered around the streets, stopping to look at everything. Yes, everything:

the street vendors, the window cleaners, the taxis, the tall skyscrapers, and the modern buildings. Everything. He stopped to watch as rushing people deposited quarters into a soda machine, fascinated at the notion of a small coin being transformed into a canned beverage with no person to affect the transaction that he could see. The technology was impressive and remarkable.

As he watched though, trying to blend in, trying to be one of these people, he noticed strange and often bizarre clothing these future people sported. Compared to his conservative 1890's attire, their clothing seemed almost perverse. Men wore jewelry. Women wore pants. It was so confusing to him. Yet, if this was the custom, and if he were to gain their trust long enough to study them, he would have to conform.

****

The clothing store was Carlisle's first stop of the afternoon. A tall, balding man, who had just enough hair for a ponytail, greeted him. The ponytail was dyed green. Like a child, Carlisle obediently followed along with anything his green haired sales clerk had in mind. He tried on various outfits, attempting to keep with the times, but Carlisle was never pleased. *Future or no future, I cannot adorn myself with these*, he thought to himself.

Finally, the sales clerk showed Carlisle a small rack of distinguished gentlemen suits and Carlisle was sent on his way in a brown twill sports coat, slacks and a cream colored shirt. Atop his head was an elegant hat. He also carried a spare suit and shirt in bag. Carlisle looked like a college professor, fitting enough, since that was his life's calling.

Next, the appropriately dressed Carlisle was introduced to a mall as he continued exploring his new world. The building was amazing in its size and it obviously drew large numbers of people from off the streets. Surely there must be something inside that was so incredible that everyone had to go in. Carlisle joined them entering the mall. He gawked in wonder at the stores...and more stores...and more stores. *This is a city within itself*, Carlisle thought. Everything caught his eyes. Trendy fashion stores with fancy displays; bookstore shelves lined with hundreds and hundreds of books; jewelry stores displaying the finest in diamonds and gold; to endless places in which people seem to congregate to obtain food. Carlisle quickly covered his eyes as he passed by a ladies lingerie store, deeming the sight inappropriate.

Walking into an electronics store, Carlisle managed to come across a touch lamp. Like a child, he watched in amazement as his very fingers ignited the light. He touched it on, he touched it off. Then back on again. Then back off again. He continued to play with it, fascinated by the new toy.

After gathering a few strange looks from the people around him, Carlisle exited the electronic store and entered a game arcade. With all of the digitized gunfire and kids maneuvering realistic machine guns, Carlisle moved as if in a war zone. He kept low and alert, dodging for fear of his life. Games assaulted him that displayed forms of monsters his mind could never conjure up. Coming across a game where two computer men dueled with swords, he watched all of the lights and movement with fascination. The computer characters moved with such fluidity. They moved like men but looked like well, he didn't know what they looked like. It was definitely something he could never had imagined. He touched the screen, trying to feel the characters. Having to deal with junkies and stoners all day, the coin lady watched Carlisle with suspicious scorn. Feeling caught, he jerked his hand away.

In a toy store, a dancing soda can arrested Carlisle's attention. He watched it, enthralled by the oddity. Then, with comical horror, he was startled when a child next to him squeezed a stuff animal and a loud noise issued forth.

In yet another electronic store, Carlisle watched with craving interest while a little boy, who knew what he was doing, worked a computer terminal, surfing the net. Carlisle watched the young child and tried to mimic his movements on his very own keyboard. However, lacking any skill or knowledge, Carlisle only succeeded in causing the computer to spew out violent noises at him. Enough fun there. 1890 had *nothing* like this. Sadly though, as far as Carlisle could see in his walking the streets, visiting the stores, and his mall experience, there had been no mention or sight of anything pertaining to Jesus thus far. This future seemed devoid of the God Who created it, yet strangely aware of the Devil who corrupted it. *Maybe I judged my friend Norris too quickly*, he mused to himself.

****

It had been quite a day and Carlisle was glad it was almost over. Exhausted, he dragged himself down the busy streets, amazed that everywhere he looked people were still going with the same intensity he observed earlier in the afternoon. On his way back to his hotel, he passed a Laundromat. He peered in the giant glass window and curiously watched people stuffing their belongings into giant drums. He had no idea what they were doing. A Hispanic man, about forty, sat behind the counter and paid a heavy amount of attention to an odd little box. Even from his vantagepoint, Carlisle could hear the odd little box spouting human voices without the benefit any person present. Carlisle figured he could fit one more oddity in before he checked in for the night so he entered the Laundromat.

"Good day to you, sir," Carlisle said, greeting the Hispanic man behind the counter.

As static overcame the frequency, the man worked on his radio, trying to get the baseball game in clearer. He talked to it in Spanish. Feeling scolded, the radio cleared up and the game came back into focus. He smiled in appreciation and started listening again, intently. So intently, in fact, he didn't respond to Carlisle who was standing on the other side of the counter admiring the radio, too.

"Pardon me. What is that device?" Carlisle asked in honest curiosity.

The man was really trying to listen to this game. "What?" he spouted out as an afterthought.

Carlisle, not sensing he was being a bother, restated his question, "That device, what is it called?"

"Huh? It's a radio, man!" The Hispanic man blurted out, trying not to interrupt the game, "Where you been?" After giving Carlisle a weird look and grumbling in Spanish, the Hispanic man went back to his intent listening.

Carlisle was still amazed by the radio, "What a fantastic way to communicate."

"SHH! Keep it down, man. There's two on and it's the bottom of the eighth."

The Laundromat attendant thought that was enough to end the conversation, but for Carlisle, it only created more questions in his pursuit of knowledge.

"Bottom of the eighth?" Carlisle raised an eyebrow, "The eighth what?"

Frustrated, the man yelled back, "The ball game man, the ball game!" Finally, he turned aside to Carlisle, "What you need?"

Carlisle began to see that the attendant wanted to be left alone. However, he felt it proper to introduce himself to his new acquaintance.

"My name is Russell Carlisle. What is your name, sir?"

The man was still distracted by the next batter, "Eddie. Eddie Martinez."

"Pleasure meeting you, Eddie," Carlisle smiled.

Carlisle really felt good about himself. He had made a new friend in this strange time.

"You need some supplies?" Eddie asked. Eddie seemed a bit rude, but Carlisle wasn't in the position to be picky about whom he talked to in the future. However, come to think of it, he *did* have a question.

Tomorrow was Sunday.

"Actually," Carlisle inquired, "I was wondering...is there a good church nearby where I can attend service in the morning?"

Eddie, never taking his attention off of the game, grabbed a raggedy phone book from under the desk and tossed it on the counter.

"Here, look one up in the Yellow Pages," he offered with no enthusiasm.

"Yellow pages?" Carlisle said aloud to himself, "Uhhh...I am not quite sure."

Eddie complained more in Spanish and then flipped to the church section in the yellow pages slapping the phone-book down in front of Carlisle.

"Right here, man," he snapped.

Carlisle tried to make sense of all the numbers and ads and strange words but it was too confusing. He decided to turn control over to Eddie, "Where do you go to church, Eddie?"

"I ain't got no time for church." Eddie left it at that.

Carlisle picked it back up, "No time for God's people? We all need accountability and encouragement from each other in the Lord. You separate yourself from a local fellowship and it is difficult to live for Jesus."

"You a preacher or something?" his tone sounded surprisingly impressed.

"No. However, I am a Professor at a Bible seminary. Eddie, why not you and I attend a service somewhere tomorrow morning?"

The brief attention that Carlisle thought he had gained of Eddie's was his, one second, the game's the next.

"Quiet, the bases are loaded," Eddie said looking back at the radio. Then, calling out to the radio, he rooted for his team, "Come on DeBottis, strike him out."

Carlisle rolled this one over in his mind wondering exactly as to its meaning, *Strike him out?*

CHAPTER SEVEN

"Church in the Twenty-first Century"

Sunday morning and Carlisle woke up with a sense of joy. Finally, something was familiar, attending a worship service at church. Everything else was so different here, very confusing and even scary at times. However, this was Sunday and Carlisle knew one thing for certain. Times change, but the Lord stays the same. A scripture even came to mind. Hebrews 13:8.

"Jesus Christ is the same yesterday, and today, and forever."

Amen, Carlisle sighed to himself. He was sure this would be a glorious day. *The Lord never changes, so why would His church?* Although Eddie was no help, too consumed with that baseball game last night, Carlisle did find a Good Samaritan in the hotel lobby who gave him directions to a Bible-believing church the night before. Armed with confidence and those directions, Carlisle easily found the church, just a short walk from his hotel. It was a very nice church with a modern appearance. The sanctuary was very spacious with polished oak pews and tinted windows. Carlisle walked through the huge double doors, took off his distinguished hat and with his Bible held close to his chest, breathed in the atmosphere he loved. It was beautiful. Marvelous. Carlisle felt he was home, feeling safe and secure in the presence of his Lord. At peace, he walked down the aisles, amidst the worshippers of the future.

He followed the flock of people into the back hall. There, he could see everyone splitting off into different Sunday school settings. Confused as to which class he should attend, he awkwardly asked a gentleman in the hall. The man was very helpful and before long, Carlisle found himself where he needed to be. He entered the class with anticipation looking forward to an enthusiastic conversation about the Bible and the things of the Lord. There were already at least twenty people there, both men and women. With chairs set in a circle, Carlisle sat in the nearest one he could find, next to a gentleman about his age. The class had yet to begin but Carlisle noticed various private conversations already going on.

Just then, a lady in her thirties, spoke up to address the class, "What time are we meeting for bargain night?" she questioned.

Bargain night? Carlisle pondered. *Some type of code the people of the future use.*

"6:30, side entrance?" A man called back.

The group muttered their "Okays" and "Sounds good" as they all nodded in agreement.

Another man spoke up, "And don't forget Tuesday night visitation."

The others, with no real interest in going, ignored the statement.

Meanwhile, Carlisle was quite confused by "bargain night" and began to listen in on the various conversations that had resumed. His eyes first moved directly across the room to two women who were doing their best to keep their voices low, but not low enough.

"Mike and Linda broke up," the first one began, "he was cheating on her."

The other gasped, adding, "I knew he was, but I didn't want to say anything."

Carlisle raised an eyebrow and continued down the row to the next conversation. Two men, dressed for golf rather than church, came into view.

"And the company's planning to go public," finished the man in a polo shirt.

The other man, sporting khakis and an alligator shirt, was quick to respond, "Get me some shares, I want in."

"I'll see what I can do," Polo Shirt replied, feeling important.

"Don't forget about me now," his eager friend seriously entreated.

Carlisle shook his head in more confusion as nothing was making sense to him. Just then, the teacher gathered the classroom together and after a couple of quick "hellos," began to speak, "Okay people, let's turn to our lesson in John chapter eight."

Carlisle smiled. *Yes, immediately*, he beamed to himself. He was ready to learn and converse. Only about half of the group even acknowledged the teacher's request and began turning to the appropriate chapter. Of course, Carlisle was the first to get there. The group however, continued to talk among themselves as if they were at a social gathering instead of in church. Even the teacher engaged in chitchat with someone nearby. Carlisle's attention was drawn to more conversations as he was trying to figure out what was so important to make everyone keep talking. He spotted two older ladies and the first was saying, "I mean, I think if you believe in God and you live a good life, how could God send you to Hell?"

Another lady, wearing very expensive clothing, calmed her, "Don't be alarmed. When kids go off to college, they sometimes get all sorts of wild notions. It happened with my son too, he'll calm down and it will pass."

Carlisle could scarcely believe his ears. What was he hearing? These were the mature Christians in the church. Of all the people in the congregation to be so misled by the world, these should be the least! Carlisle was shaken. Something Norris said to him that day immediately came to mind.

"Satan, our adversary, is not against good morals. He is opposed to Jesus Christ. Thus, Satan is using the teaching of good morals alone to deceive people into thinking that they can live a good life to merit heaven.

As Carlisle continued his eye sweep of the room, two men in jeans and denim shirts broke Carlisle from his thoughts.

"It's our coach," one denim man said in frustration, "he doesn't know basketball. He's zone happy and he won't let the kids run."

Agreeing with him, his friend added, "Yeah, but we'll never get him out of there. He's the Principal's nephew."

The first threatened, "They better do something or I'm going to stop going to the games."

Concentrating on those conversations, Carlisle was a bit startled when he realized the man sitting next to him was staring curiously at Carlisle's Bible. Offering a friendly smile, Carlisle spoke, "And what has the Lord been speaking to you through His Word?"

The man paused for a minute, as if contemplating his question, and then held up his Bible, "Have you ever noticed the printing quality and the binding on these Bibles?"

Carlisle had no reply.

****

Class was over, and Carlisle was very disappointed at the lack of depth and spiritual conversation during Sunday school class. He decided maybe they were tired and their zeal for the Lord would show during the worship service. The song leader was already at the pulpit making announcements as Carlisle quietly took the nearest seat he could find. Ready to worship, Carlisle thoroughly enjoyed himself during the singing time, which followed. He sang loudly and unashamedly of the Lord who saved his soul, not realizing he was drawing attention from those nearby. He eagerly awaited the sermon when the pastor entered the pulpit. The pastor, not the most eloquent speaker, seemed sincere and started sharing a message from the book of Ephesians; continuing a teaching series he had begun several weeks ago. Carlisle soaked in every word, following along in his Bible and turning to the various Bible passages quoted from the man of God. However, it was at this time that Carlisle began to sense something in the air and began looking around. He noticed he was about the only one truly listening; about the only one who was feeling the joy of the Lord; about the only one being refreshed from hearing God's Word taught. In fact, to his view, the church of the twenty-first century was....

Bored.

TIME CHANGER

He saw people checking their watches, doodling on their bulletins, teenagers giggling with each another, a young couple enraptured in love, too tuned into one another to pay attention to the pastor. Some people appeared to be...sleeping! There was a core group of people who were paying attention, but a small core at that. It seemed to Carlisle that the majority of the congregation wished they were somewhere else. Carlisle grimaced.

****

After the service dismissed, almost everyone made a straight line for the church exits. Carlisle, feeling out of place, walked outside and observed the mad dash continue to the parking lot. He was feeling very perplexed, but also wondering how he could better fit in. After all, he was only going to be here for a few short days and he did not plan on spending his limited time in the future alone. Then, he spotted the lady that addressed the Sunday school class earlier. He remembered she was the one that asked the questions about bargain night. He decided he would try to make sense of it all.

"Beg your pardon, madam," Carlisle asked, tipping his hat, as he approached the lady. "In our Sunday school class earlier, you spoke about a...'bargain night'? Could you please tell me what you meant?"

The lady, kind in demeanor, looked at Carlisle with a curious stare thinking he was putting her on. Finally, it clicked that he was sincere and she quickly explained, "Oh! We're all going to watch a movie tomorrow night at the theater."

"A movie?" Carlisle was careful to pronounce the word, not wanting to say it wrong.

"Why don't you come with us? You'll enjoy it. It's half price. Just meet us outside, right here."

Carlisle nodded, accepting the invitation, "Could you also tell me what Tuesday night visitation is?"

"That's when people from the church go and visit prospective members."

Carlisle smiled thinking to himself, *What a lovely sentiment.* The lady was quick to add, "but not too many people show up for that."

About that time, the lady's husband, obviously in a hurry to leave, came up behind her. He tugged her elbow as he passed by, "Come on honey, let's go. Dinner's going to burn."

The husband continued to make his way for the car as the lady snapped back waving him off, "I'm coming." She then turned to Carlisle and spoke kindly again, "Well, hope to see you tomorrow night."

Carlisle tipped his hat once more as the lady left and followed after her husband.

CHAPTER EIGHT

"Something's Wrong"

It was early Sunday afternoon and Carlisle was still disappointed over his first experience with the church of the twenty-first century. He had wandered from the church to a nearby park and began a leisurely stroll, admiring this beautiful Sunday. He then realized he still hadn't eaten anything. He stopped and noticed a man selling food, a hot dog vendor. The vendor was already in the process of serving a couple of customers as Carlisle happened by.

He approached the vendor and looked at the selection on the menu. After deducing a solid order, he ventured, "I think I would like to try one of those..." he observed the sign, just to make sure he pronounced the ridiculous name right, "Hot dogs?"

"With relish and mustard?" the vendor, all business, replied automatically.

Carlisle stepped back. *I should have known it would not have been that simple.* "Is this customary?"

"Whazzat?" the vendor said, not in the mood.

Carlisle decided to just be brave, "Eh...er, yes. Yes, I do."

"Something to drink?"

Carlisle looked again at his choices and nothing was familiar. He saw bottle after bottle of soft drinks and fruit punches with names he couldn't pronounce.

"Water?" He replied, anxiously.

****

Carlisle took his treat, content with the transaction, and found a park bench where he could enjoy his "nutritious" meal. However, all was not well in the park. Something was wrong. From the bushes, some children were watching Carlisle. Carlisle set his hot dog down on the bench beside him, removed his hat, and closed his eyes to bless his food. After a sufficient prayer, Carlisle opened his eyes ready to enjoy this future delicacy, when he realized his hot dog was missing. He quickly glanced around the park and saw a young girl running away with his meal, with her friends racing behind her. Flabbergasted over the audacity of the young thief, Carlisle donned his hat and quickly pursued.

"Excuse me!" He called out, realizing he was getting slower in his older age. The children scattered as Carlisle continued to chase the young girl through the park, trying not to let his age show. Finally, somehow, he managed to catch her and grabbed her by the arm turning the youngster gently towards him. He was shocked to find that the girl, blonde with very hard eyes and smudges of mud on her face, was no more than eleven years old. He pitied her and wanted to help, but that did not excuse what she had done.

So, very practically, he informed her, "Young lady, you have stolen my meal. Why would you do such a thing?"

The girl was very cynical and jaded for such a young age. She blew off the incident and backed down, now that she'd been caught red handed. "I was just playing around," she lied.

"I would be very happy to purchase your very own if you are hungry and need something to eat."

The girl was offended and didn't feel she needed this stuffy old guy's pity. She shoved the hot dog back to its rightful owner, "Here, take your dog."

Carlisle took his meal, but was still not pleased with the girl's actions, or her intent. He persisted, "This is unacceptable young lady. You do know that stealing is a sin?"

"Yeah, says who?"

The shock of her statement knocked Carlisle off balance enough for the little girl to jerk her arm out of Carlisle's hand and run away. He could only stand behind, hot dog in hand, and finally admit to himself that something was wrong with this place.

He was wrong.

"The Lord says," he uttered quietly into the air.

****

After eating his hot dog, but not enjoying it nearly as much as he thought he would, Carlisle went back to the mall. He started to realize things were not as happy as they appeared. In fact, it seemed that the people of this time were disillusioned, believing themselves that everything was fine. Carlisle was an outsider though and knew different. He was determined to share his findings with them.

Again he stood, at first afar, in front of the lingerie store, looking at the lifeless mannequins modeling the risqué wardrobe. His expression was frozen as he watched two boys, gaping at the clothing, or lack thereof, giggling between themselves and running off. Seeing this, Carlisle became even more disturbed.

These people have no shame, he pondered within. *They have no limits.* This time though, Carlisle was going to have to do something about it. With a sense of heroism, he marched boldly into the lingerie store. Trying to evade the provocative clothing through a gauntlet of lace, he made his way untouched and approached the young man behind the counter.

"Excuse me, young man," Carlisle began, maintaining his bravado, "May I speak with the proprietor of this establishment?"

Confused at first, the college graduate finally caught on, "You mean the owner? He's not here, but I'm his son. Can I help you?"

His son? Carlisle gasped. His own father had once tried to bring Carlisle into the family business, but that was something honorable like shoe making. How could a father submit his child to seeing scantily clad women images all day? Carlisle felt the need to save this boy.

"It is in regards to the women's night garments in the front window display over there."

The young man looked over at the display, not getting the point. He looked back at Carlisle joking, "Well, I don't think they would look that good on you."

Carlisle was taken aback, "Beg your pardon?"

The young man laughed, "Just kidding, mister. I know. I know. Your wife will look great in one of these outfits and you want me to give you a special deal, right? I think we can work something out."

As soon as Carlisle got the image of Helen in those clothes out of his mind, he reaffirmed his business, "No, sir. Nothing like that, at all." Carlisle recomposed himself and leaned into the young man, as if breaking some shocking news to him. "I do not know how this will be taken by you, young sir, but I am sure that this manner of dress arouses sinful passions in the customers as they pass by." Then, just when the young man thought Carlisle couldn't lean in any closer, he did, "Especially the young boys."

"What?" The young man said, not getting it.

"I am sure it is displeasing to the Lord."

The young man took two steps back and thought it over. A co-worker had noticed the conversation and had come closer. Figuring Carlisle for some religious loon, the young man handled this with as much care as his twenty-three years allowed for.

"I see," he nodded, trying to sound serious about the matter, "Sir, I appreciate your opinion and I'll let my father know, but this is the first complaint we've ever had about this. For the most part, people just don't have a problem with this sort of thing."

The young man felt that he had sufficiently handled Carlisle's complaint and turned to conversing with the co-worker who was now standing behind the counter. Carlisle was left alone in his thoughts and walked away, back into the mall corridor. As he left, he turned and looked back through the window hidden from view, but where he could still see the young man talking to a couple co-workers. They were laughing, and Carlisle knew it was at his expense.

CHAPTER NINE

"Eddie: Round One"

Exhausted again after another day of walking the streets and exploring every store in site, Carlisle walked back to the Laundromat to check on his "friend", Eddie. He was still trying to sort through everything that had happened to him these past twenty-four hours. As he walked through the door, the bells jingled, declaring his presence and Eddie spotted him right away from behind the counter. The place wasn't crowded.

"Hey," Eddie called out, friendly, "The preacher got some new threads."

Eddie's smile was big, but the expression on Carlisle's face quickly told Eddie that he had no idea what "threads" meant. Carlisle shook his head shrugging his shoulders. Eddie served as translator, "Clothes, man, you know?"

The light visibly went on in Carlisle's head. He smiled and nodded. Eddie mumbled something to himself in

Spanish, then banged the radio one time in hopes of getting better reception.

"You enjoy listening to that box?" Carlisle inquired.

"Eh, we won last night," Eddie beamed with pride.

"Which is good, right?" Carlisle said trying to fit in.

"If we win tonight, we tied for first place," Eddie happily announced.

As Eddie turned to listen to the game, Carlisle began to think about Eddie and his spiritual state. Although very disillusioned and taken by what he had seen in the twenty-first century thus far, especially within the church, it didn't mean all was bad. Jesus was still real and God was still extending His grace to save people from their sin giving them eternal life. *Did Eddie really know what Jesus was all about?* Carlisle knew he would not feel right if he left this time without bringing it up.

"Do you think much about Jesus, Eddie?" Carlisle sincerely asked.

"What's that?" Eddie didn't seem to hear, as his attention was still on the game.

"Jesus," Carlisle repeated. "Do you ever think about Jesus?"

Eddie defended himself, "Hey, I go to church every Christmas and Easter."

"Yes, but you understand that going to church does not save us from our sin?"

Carlisle's comment didn't seem to register with Eddie, who was still defending himself, "And I ain't done no time in the slammer like most of my amigos."

"Slammer?" Carlisle asked, trying to understand.

"Jail man, jail! I thought *my* English bad," Eddie went back to listening to the radio but Carlisle wasn't giving up that easily.

"Jesus wants to give us eternal life, Eddie."

"Shhh," Eddie said, ignoring Carlisle, "Jimmy Lincoln just got a double with two on. The score is now three to two."

Carlisle persisted, "But we must first enter into a personal relationship with Him as our Lord."

Eddie's mind was still on the game. "I can't hear."

Now Carlisle was getting frustrated. Here he was trying to talk to Eddie about the most important issue in life and Eddie was not giving him any attention.

"Do you want eternal life, Eddie?" Carlisle raised his voice.

"Come on man," Eddie pleaded, talking to the radio, "Get a hit."

"Eddie, I am attempting to talk to you about Jesus!"

"Look, preacher," Eddie stopped with his game to defend his honor, "I never shot no one and I don't cheat on my wife. Eddie Martinez is a good guy. You ask anyone."

Carlisle was once again taken by Eddie's remark, a remark very similar to the one he heard earlier in the day during the Sunday school class. *There it is again. The claim for morality. A person thinking that all they have to do is live a good life to earn heaven, just as Norris had said.*

A loud cheer emitted from the radio breaking into Carlisle's thoughts and drawing Eddie's applause, "Eh! We got another run! We up four to two." He turned to Carlisle, "Hey, you're good luck, preacher. Stick around."

Carlisle half smiled, but inside was disappointed. He politely excused himself but knew this wasn't over. While Eddie seemed obsessed with who was winning the baseball game, he was completely oblivious that two teams were also competing over the greatest prize of all, his eternal soul. He was missing the supernatural battle going on between the Lord of Hosts and prince of darkness. Jesus and Satan. Truth versus Deception.

It's a battle, too, because Deception is a fierce warrior.

****

As Carlisle entered his hotel room, his exchange with Eddie was still on his mind. *There seems to be so many distractions.* Carlisle longed for his days when technology and progress didn't get in the way of Jesus. Now, man's self-sufficiency had become his god. His idol. Carlisle took a moment to pray to the Lord for Eddie. Carlisle was a sensitive and sincere man. When he prayed for people, he truly interceded for them, expecting nothing for himself in return.

However, he wasn't always so selfless.

Carlisle grew up in a very conservative Christian home. He was a well-respected, well-mannered teenager who was held in high regards with most in his community. It seemed that Carlisle had a knack for getting things his way. He had a way of manipulating people with his strong personality, although, maybe not always on purpose. Carlisle was active in his local church and had many opportunities to speak in front of small groups to expound on the Scriptures and "enlighten" others with his Bible knowledge. Despite his seeming understanding of the truth, young Carlisle was *not* a true believer. The young man was deceived. It was obvious he knew all the facts about Christ and acknowledged them, but he lived for himself. He did things that would only advance *his* purposes and career, many times doing so under the guise of serving the Lord.

One night, when he was only nineteen and before he

had met Helen, Carlisle, with some friends, attended a gathering at a neighbor's house to hear a travelling speaker. There were only eleven people sitting in front of the fireplace that night. While most were there to sincerely welcome this visitor, Carlisle and his friends had other motives. They knew this man was considered to be very knowledgeable in the Scriptures and they were hoping to discuss with him some of the more controversial issues pertaining to Reformed Theology. Carlisle and his friends had heard of certain beliefs that this man held and disagreed with them. Even though they would never admit to seeking to argue, they were open in their desire for a heated discussion. Yes, Carlisle and his friends were certain that they could teach this man a thing or two.

That night, before the discussion began, the man of the house had asked the speaker to share a brief testimony with his small group. Carlisle and his friends, with their smug looks, were ready to discredit this man of God. They were hoping for inconsistencies that they could later follow up on in the discussion to follow.

The man, humble yet confident, stood to face the few gathered and said, "I want to ask you a question tonight. Who are you trusting in to give you eternal life? Are you trusting in your intellect, in your ability to discuss the Scriptures, in your ability to intimidate others with your Bible knowledge? Are you comparing yourself to others, seeing yourself as more superior? Or, are you trusting in Jesus Christ to save you from your sin, putting no confidence in yourself? Philippians 3:3 says that the true circumcision worship God in the Spirit, rejoice in Christ Jesus and have no confidence in the flesh. So, my friends, I ask you tonight. In your life, who are you trusting, Christ or yourself?"

After only those few short, but powerful words, the man of God quietly took his seat by the fireplace with the others and that was it. No sermon. No great theological lesson. Carlisle's friends began to whisper under their breath, a bit disappointed at the brief word. Carlisle, though, was oddly silent. The Spirit of God had so convicted him of what had just been said that Carlisle began to weep openly. He knew, right then, that he had been trusting in himself and his knowledge instead of Jesus and His sacrifice. Russell Carlisle humbly and unashamedly got up, approached the man of God and asked him to join him in the next room to pray with him.

In the next room, bowed down before the sovereignty of the Father, Carlisle confessed his self-sufficiency to the Lord and cried out to Jesus for the saving of his soul. Russell Carlisle became a true believer that evening and was changed forever.

That was many years ago. Since then, Carlisle had retained his strong personality, but now there was a new-found softness and sincerity that replaced the self-serving and coldness in his heart. In fact, it was this new love, one that could only have come from above, that brought he and Helen together. Through the years, Carlisle always kept in mind the height from which he had fallen, never taking his blessings for granted. He was truly saved by grace and no longer trusting in himself. Now he was compelled to share the wonderful gift of salvation with others, just as the man of God had brought to him so long ago.

So his concern about Eddie's spiritual welfare was an honest one. No longer did Russell Carlisle seek to help others only to help himself or to appear righteous in the eyes of men. No, that Carlisle was gone.

Lying back on his bed at the Excelsior Hotel, Carlisle

reached for his Bible and began to read. He was still troubled in his spirit, though, and unable to concentrate. This new time and this new place were so different, and Carlisle was indecisive as to what he could do to influence it. Just then, Norris' final words called out to him from the past.

"One more piece of instruction. Look up a gentleman by the name of Mitchell Bain. You will find him at the public library. He knows me but not where I am from. He will be helpful to you."

Carlisle closed his eyes, just to rest them for a moment before continuing his reading, but fell off to sleep.

CHAPTER TEN

"A Friend in the Future"

The public library was open the next morning, and Carlisle made it a priority to go there first. Finding Mitchell Bain wasn't hard. The secretary at the front desk was most helpful and before he knew it, Carlisle was sitting across the desk from the man that Norris said could help him. Mitchell Bain was a tall, slender, distinguished looking gentleman in his sixties. Carlisle was excited to meet him and their mutual friendship with Norris began the conversation.

"So how is Norris?" Mitchell stated from behind his desk. "I haven't seen him for awhile."

Carlisle smiled and nodded, "He is doing quite well." Thinking it best to test this new acquaintance, Carlisle questioned, "Can you tell me what you know of our mutual friend?"

Mitchell thought about it for a moment and recalled, "Well, he came in here one day, about six months ago, and we began talking. Nice man. Norris is a Bible professor, but I'm sure you know that."

Nodding, Carlisle smiled, "Yes, I too am a professor. We are colleagues in fact."

Mitchell, intrigued and a bit surprised, leaned forward with curiosity, "Oh really? Well, how did that experiment of his work out?"

Carlisle was caught off guard and began to sweat. *How did he know?* "Excuse me?" Carlisle meekly replied.

"That experiment. He said he was part of some science experiment and so he couldn't tell me where he was from or what, exactly, he was doing here." Mitchell stopped to think back to his time with Norris, "He seemed very out of place, though. Like he was from another culture or something."

Mitchell continued to chew on that for a moment. Carlisle broke from the topic, laughing nervously, "Yes, well, both of us have been away from *this* society for quite sometime."

Seeming to forget the "experiment" topic, Mitchell moved on to other memories of Norris, "We spent a lot of time discussing spiritual matters."

Carlisle raised a curious eyebrow, intrigued. Feeling some strange need for secrecy, Carlisle leaned in closer and began to whisper, lest this information should fall into the wrong hands, "Yes, like Norris, I too am also interested in knowing the spiritual state of the times."

Mitchell Bain let out an exasperated sigh and leaned back in his chair, "Where do I start?" Obviously, the subject was a sore one with him.

Carlisle began to relay his discoveries, hopeful to find an explanation. "Yesterday, I attended a worship service at the large church on Main Street."

Mitchell shook his head, recognizing the place, "Yes, I am familiar with it."

Carlisle felt just horrible for having to break the bad news to Mitchell, "Hopefully, this will not be offensive to your kind ears, but by my observation, there seemed to be a boredom with the entire service, with the praise hymns and the hearing of God's Word. Everything."

Mitchell took a breath, preparing to admit the short-comings of the present day church, "Mr. Carlisle, the Church in general, in my opinion, that is, if you would like to hear it?"

Carlisle was on the edge of his seat. Finally some answers, "Yes, please."

"The Church is in a terrible state."

Before Mitchell could continue, however, a female's voice came over the intercom.

"Excuse me, Mitchell. Sorry to interrupt. Line two. The state office."

Mitchell thanked the secretary and Carlisle was amazed at the "invention." Mitchell, reaching for some papers, turned to Carlisle, apologetic, "Excuse me, Mr. Carlisle."

"Please. Call me Russell," Carlisle smiled.

Mitchell smiled back, honored, "Russell, sorry about this. I've been waiting for this call." Carlisle nodded, disappointed. Mitchell picked back up, "Look, I'd love to chat with you some more. Maybe you could come by tomorrow about one o'clock, that's when I take lunch. We'll have more time to talk then."

Carlisle nodded as Mitchell went for the phone. He left the office, slightly bowing and offered one last formality, "Very kind of you, sir. I shall look forward to it."

Carlisle left just as Mitchell picked up the phone and connected to his call.

****

The sun was beginning to set and night was fast approaching. Carlisle reasoned he still had a couple of hours before bargain night and found it best to obtain a meal before the event.

He entered a diner and took a seat in an out of the way booth in the corner of the restaurant. A jukebox slept directly behind him, as Carlisle tried to make sense out of the menu. After a couple of minutes, Carlisle's waitress arrived while a group of teens with a fresh batch of quarters approached to awaken the jukebox. The waitress was not into formalities.

"What'll ya have?"

Carlisle wasn't on that page of the conversation, yet. He was not used to the direct business customs of the future. "Hello, madam," he smiled.

The waitress wasn't fazed, "What'll ya have?"

Carlisle frowned. *Very well, then.* He examined his menu one last time, "Yes, I'll have this selection…number two?"

Upon ordering, the waitress yelled to the kitchen in the back, startling Carlisle who was unprepared from such conduct from a lady. "Number two!" she screamed. Immediately turning to Carlisle, she returned to business, "Something to drink?"

Carlisle recovered from the shock and weakly replied, "Water?"

The waitress wrote it down. However, just as the waitress was about to walk off, the teenagers' first tune began to play on the jukebox, causing it to explode with a loud, grating modern day rock song, assaulting Carlisle's ears.

Carlisle, thinking the waitress was loud enough, almost fell out of his seat at this explosion of noise. He grabbed his ears, attempting to locate the source of the torment.

"What is that dreadful noise?!"

The waitress watched him, unsure, "What noise?"

Carlisle spun around to the jukebox, deeming that infernal machine the culprit. He pointed madly, accusing, "*That* noise!"

"What? The music?"

Carlisle was wide-eyed and disturbed, still covering his ears from the noise. The waitress walked away. Carlisle, still in shock, managed to mumble, "Music?"

CHAPTER ELEVEN

"Bargain Night"

At least twenty-five people were present for the bargain night adventure. Laughter was everywhere and everyone was joining in the fun. Carlisle though, was nervous and kept his distance. Nervous because he had never traveled in a vehicle before, keeping his distance because he did not want to intrude, knowing he didn't fit in. Every conversation he initiated thus far had ended in confusion. He had no idea how to talk to these people. He felt like a foreigner in what he thought was still his own country.

How could so much change in one hundred years? He wondered. It was like civilization had been catapulted in an entirely new direction. The rapid progress of this world was astounding, if not a little scary. Carlisle was sure all of this advancement must play a part in the ushering in of end time events and the Second Coming. He was greatly anticipating his next visit with Mitchell Bain who he hoped would be able to provide some answers.

People started boarding the bus and Carlisle was the last reluctant passenger to board. He had no idea what this thing was or how it operated. However, everyone else seemed to be at ease. He stepped on the bus and took a seat in the rear, away from the others. The driver, all smiles, checked to see if everybody was there, then closed the door, sealing it tight with a squeak. They were ready to go.

As the bus pulled away, passerbies could see the bug-eyed expression of an enchanted and fearful man named Russell Carlisle staring out the back window, trying to understand his circumstance.

****

Minutes later, the bus pulled into the theater parking lot. The ride was incredible to Carlisle who had never felt so much energy from a machine since...since...well, since *the* machine. The machine that brought him to the future. It was terrifying at first, but by the time the bus stopped at the cinema complex, Carlisle was more calm and felt as if he had accomplished something. He was still cautious though and happy he had made it safely to the destination. The parking lot was loading up quickly, as there was already lots of activity. Carlisle wanted to stay in the bus away from all the bright lights of the cinema and the roaring chatter of the teenage crowd. As he departed the bus, the bus driver noticed how uneasy he was.

"What's wrong mister? You act as if you never rode in a bus before," he said jokingly.

Carlisle smiled at the bus driver and then let off a small sigh of relief as he stepped on solid ground again. His group was already on their way across the parking lot, so Carlisle had to hustle to catch up to them.

The cinema was absolutely breathtaking to Carlisle as he entered seeing all of the lights and the beautiful upholstery. It almost looked like one of the grand theaters from his own time, which made him feel a little better. The feeling didn't last long though, as ensuing chaos and confusion pushed all familiarity aside. The sights inside the theater were worse than that outside. Teenagers were running and laughing and shoving handfuls of strange puffy white things into their mouths. In fact, Carlisle noticed the place seemed to be run by teenagers. He wondered why they weren't home studying or *something*. Anything other than loitering about. Where were their parents? Were the children of the future just allowed to roam at their own discretion without the guidance of caring parents? He shook his head once more. Then, he realized that shaking his head was something he had been doing quite often as of late.

His group's wait in line was relatively short and they received their tickets. Carlisle noticed his group chose a movie with the letters "PG" and the number "13" on it. *Argh,* he thought, *more code.* After receiving their tickets, the group moved through the halls of the theater, passing by several movie posters. Each fascinated Carlisle, even though some looked quite scary to him. They entered theater number nine and all sat together. The room was dark and Carlisle was surprisingly calm. He concluded if he could not see them, they could not see him, either. For a brief moment, he felt all right, there. The lights began to dim, something Carlisle didn't think was possible, and the large red curtain at the front of the theater slowly opened. As the screen came alive with motion and the room filled with sound, Carlisle sat back amazed, and felt more comfortable. This was going to be great!

****

Twenty minutes into the movie, after the mob of people had been herded off into their respective cinemas and the employees were the only ones in the lobby; Carlisle came running out, pale and panicked.

"You must stop the movie!" he cried, waving his arms as if the building were on fire, "STOP THE MOVIE!!"

All of the employees came to an abrupt halt, baffled but concerned. Carlisle went on, "The man in the movie just blasphemed the name of the LORD JESUS CHRIST! There must be some mistake. You must stop the movie! THIS IS AN ABOMINATION!!!"

The employees could only stare at this crazy, strange man as they tried to suppress their laughter.

CHAPTER TWELVE

"The Suspicion"

After the movie, Carlisle was invited, along with a group of others, back to Rex and Ann's house for refreshments. This was the couple that proposed the bargain night outing to the Sunday school class. Nine people sat around the dining room table enjoying sandwiches and soft drinks. Carlisle did not return to watch the rest of the film. He waited in the lobby for an hour and half until the rest of his group reemerged. No one noticed he was missing.

Carlisle, sitting at one end of the table, was still considerably shaken by the bargain night experience, "I just cannot overcome how this man was allowed to blaspheme the name of the Lord during the movie."

"It's not that big of a deal, Carlisle," Tom, Rex's best friend, replied candidly. "It's only a movie."

Carlisle defended, "Yes, but to defame the glorious and holy name of Jesus."

Rex entered the fray. "It was a moral film. The guy

went back with his wife in the end."

"But to speak so blatantly against the name of Jesus," Carlisle replied, unable to let it go.

Rex chimed again, "Don't take it so seriously, it's only entertainment."

Carlisle still contested, "Yes, but the name of the Lord?"

"Look, buddy," Tom's coldness was showing through, "There're a lot worse films we could have gone to see."

Unlike the others, Russell Carlisle had not yet "accepted" the entertainment of the day as the norm. "Seems to me, better not to attend at all if there is no more of a godly selection," he quickly replied.

Rex, his carefree smile bordering on mocking, leaned over to Tom whispering, "This guy must be one of those legalists who thinks all movies are sinful."

Tom had a big laugh.

"Pardon me?" replied Carlisle, thinking he was being addressed.

Ann reached over to Carlisle and patted his arm to get his attention, "Oh, don't mind them." She quickly changed the subject, "So, Mr. Carlisle, where are you from?"

Carlisle bit his lower lip. After sitting here having a moral discussion on the wrongs of the entertainment business, Carlisle felt like a hypocrite knowing he might have to lie...a little.

"From here, originally," he said quite truthfully, "Though, I have been living away for quite sometime."

"Whereabouts?" Kate asked.

"Well," Carlisle said, feeling the butterflies taking flight in his stomach, "I really cannot disclose the location."

"Out of the country?" Kate persisted.

"I will tell you this much. It is in another time zone." *Is that lying?* Carlisle debated to himself. "I have been conducting some experiments," Carlisle let slip.

"You're a scientist?!" Kate's eyes were huge.

Through a nervous smile, Carlisle tried to divulge enough information to satisfy this woman's curiosity, yet without revealing his true identity. "No. Actually, I am really part of the experiment. I am a Bible professor by trade. I teach Science and its relation to the Scriptures as well as Church History at Grace Bible Seminary."

"Grace Bible Seminary?" Ann's face was twisted in confusion, "I've never heard of it."

Carlisle offered, "It is located at the corner of 34th and Eighth streets."

Tom, who had been listening in, was not amused with this new guy and kept a suspicious eye on him. "There's a mall located there," Tom's tone was sharp and discrediting.

Of course! How could I have been so careless? Carlisle was always quick to open his mouth to "enlighten" the masses back home, but that was back home in 1890. Here, in this time, things needed to be different. He could not ramble on about things he knew from his own time. Maybe he should just keep quiet and stop talking himself into these corners.

Kate came to the rescue, after throwing her husband a dirty look, "Ann teaches Science at the high school."

"Yes," Ann added enthusiastically, "I'd love to have you come speak to my class."

"No," Carlisle responded with a kind and shy smile, "I don't think I can do that. Besides, I will only be here for a couple more days."

"Oh, you must come," Ann persisted, "The students would enjoy it. You can tell us more about your experiments."

Carlisle was running out of excuses, "I have no transportation," he said laughing nervously.

"I'll be glad to pick you up," Kate said smiling into his eyes, offering to solve the problem.

Carlisle had to give in, "It will be my pleasure."

He and the two ladies continued to discuss the event as Tom and Rex watched the new addition to their group. They studied Carlisle and whispered between themselves.

"There's something strange about this Carlisle guy," Tom said leaning towards Rex, never taking his eyes off Carlisle. "I don't think he's involved in any experiment. It's a cover for something,"

"Drugs?" Rex was honestly curious.

"Maybe. Why don't you run the computer on him tomorrow at the station."

"Gotcha," Rex nodded.

"Let's see what we find out about our new friend here."

Tom watched as Carlisle laughed with his and Rex's wives. He didn't trust this guy. More importantly, he didn't understand this guy and Tom made it a rule that anything he didn't understand, he tore down. He attended church, but he was not a man of faith. He was a man of action and prosperity who would do almost anything to make a buck. His very successful real estate business had been shady to say the least. He was a man of influence and usually got things his way. He was no one to mess with. Rex, his friend and comrade in various schemes, was also well off, thanks to Tom. He worked at the local police station and knew what was happening in this city. Tom used Rex, mostly as an informant, but Rex didn't mind. The two had made a great deal of money together and they made a good team. Carlisle would be no match for them.

CHAPTER THIRTEEN

"Stranger by the Minute"

The close call at Rex and Ann's house was...tense. It reminded Carlisle how dangerous his entire trip was. Not only dangerous, but also lonely, as he was compelled to live in secret. Carlisle stared out the window of his hotel room. He saw a number of rebellious teens loitering on the darkened streets below with no one to watch them, no one to correct them should they get out of hand. He worried for them, concerned for their well being and the destiny of their souls. Everything was so different here, so alien. But then, in this place and time, *Carlisle* was the alien. Depressed and dismayed, he desperately wanted to go back home.

****

Tom's real estate office, the biggest in town, was swarming with activity the next morning. Tom led the pack in his dedication and fervor. Concentrating hard, drowning out all the noise, he focused on his paper work, working hard on his next deal. The phone rang, and he reluctantly picked it up. He was only half listening, still interested in his paper work.

"Tom Sharp," he answered, mechanically.

"It's me," Rex's voice came through on the other end. Suddenly, Tom wasn't as interested in his paper work anymore. Rex continued, "I ran that check on Russell Carlisle and found nothing. According to our database, he doesn't exist."

"What?" Tom found that hard to believe.

"I even ran an international on him. No record of Carlisle."

"He must be using an alias, then."

"Maybe," Rex admitted.

"This is strange."

Rex offered more, "I did find something interesting, though. I checked out Grace Bible Seminary. You know, the one Carlisle said he worked at?"

"The one located in the middle of Mid Town Mall?" Tom's laugh was bitter and mean.

"That's the one. Well, it seems there used to be a seminary in that exact location. It moved across state back in '51. And there *was* a Russell Carlisle employed at the seminary as a professor."

Tom was confused, "I thought you just told me he didn't exist."

"There's one catch, though. *This* Russell Carlisle's been dead since 1936."

Tom lost his breath for a moment, a strange feeling of vertigo swept over him. There had to be a reasonable explanation. "1936. It can't be the same guy," he commented.

"I told you I found something interesting," added Rex.

"This isn't making any sense." A plan pulled itself together in Tom's mind, "What time is Carlisle scheduled to be at Ann's school today?"

"Eleven o'clock."

"I think we need to pay Carlisle's hotel room a little visit. I'll find out where my wife's picking him up."

Rex caught on quickly and smiled to himself. This was their town and no one was going to get in without them knowing it. These two made it their self appointed duty to know everyone's dirty little secrets. To be in on everything. Nothing was going to get past them.

****

It was eleven o'clock. Ann had just finished telling her high school class of juniors what little she knew of Carlisle's history and his involvement with the sciences and, more importantly, his involvement in a science experiment. After the details, Ann, with a smile, stood aside and gave Carlisle the floor. The kids seemed, at least, a little interested in what Carlisle had to say. Carlisle had thought he might be apprehensive, especially with so much at stake. The moment he took the floor though, he felt at home being in a classroom again.

A girl in the back raised her hand and spoke before given permission, "Can you tell us a little more about the experiment you're working on?"

"Uh...not yet, for I am still observing. Scientists are supposed to observe everything they can first, record their observations, and *then* make public their findings."

A sarcastic young man, obviously the spokesperson for the group, was quick to offer, "You need some help, man? I'd be glad to skip school."

The class laughed. Carlisle smiled, amused. With a thoughtful look, Carlisle turned to Ann, who was now standing off to the side, and addressed her, "Are you familiar with the works of John Anderson? He lived in the late 1800s. Brilliant mind. He published some valuable information about the art of science and experimentation."

Sharing John, Norris' father, with this new generation gave Carlisle a warm feeling inside. John Anderson's writings had meant so much to Carlisle; it felt like a father passing down a cherished pocket watch to a son.

Ann struggled in thought for a moment trying to recall the name, "John Anderson, I don't believe I've heard of him. We'll have to locate his material."

"Please do," Carlisle urged with a smile. "His discoveries are fascinating. The best element about Anderson's work is that he relates everything to the Bible."

The entire class went dead quiet, immediately. Carlisle rambled on, "Remember students, if any scientific record contradicts the Bible, then the scientific finding is in error. The Scriptures are never wrong."

Ann tried to motion to Carlisle, urging him to stop, without trying to call a lot of attention to it. However, Carlisle, feeling very comfortable and at ease, had slipped back into teacher mode. He was oblivious his discussion had raised eyebrows.

"Mr. Carlisle..." Ann said softly.

Carlisle was on a roll. He could feel that urge to pick up a stick of chalk and apply it to the chalkboard coming along. "God's Holy Word is so trustworthy. It's amazing how it has recorded scientific facts hundreds of years before science ever discovered them and with one hundred percent accuracy!"

"Mr. Carlisle," Ann was a little more forceful now.

Carlisle completely surrendered to his teaching nature and began to pace, lecturing now. He still did not hear Ann's protest. "The Holy Scripture, students, is your most reliable science book. Always."

"MR. CARLISLE!" Ann yelled, loud enough that it startled everyone and stopped Carlisle dead in his tracks. He looked at Ann, not knowing what went wrong. With a stern and almost angry look on her sweet face, she motioned for Carlisle to join her outside the classroom. Feeling a little confused he followed her. As soon as the two were gone, the students immediately broke into chatter discussing the incident among them.

Outside, Ann seemed hurt, "Mr. Carlisle, this is a public school. You can't talk about religion in class."

Carlisle was honestly confused. "I was not talking about religion. I was simply mentioning the Bible."

"This school has rules. No religious views can be expressed to the students. Do you want me to lose my job?"

Carlisle saw that Ann was really upset, even though he felt he did nothing wrong. He humbly apologized to her, never intending to hurt her. She thanked him for coming and re-entered her classroom leaving Carlisle standing in the hall alone, more befuddled than ever. *Teachers can no longer use the Bible as the most reliable source?*

****

While Carlisle was defending his faith at the high school, Tom and Rex were searching his hotel room. There wasn't much to search. Rex flung the closet door open only to find two sets of clothes, and one of those was the set that Carlisle had worn when he first arrived.

"Carlisle doesn't mess with a lot of luggage when he travels," Rex snickered.

Tom was more serious. He was busy checking in the bathroom and looking through Carlisle's toiletries. He found only a handful of items and all of those brand new. Tom then rummaged through every drawer, determined to find something suspicious. However, he couldn't find anything. Not just anything suspicious, but not *any*thing. No suitcases. No extra clothes. No keys. "If he is hustling drugs, they're not here," Tom was prompted to say.

Rex was now holding up the 1890 clothes to his body imagining himself in them. Tom, ever relentless in his pursuit, continued to look until finally he came across Carlisle's Bible in the top drawer of the nightstand, the one Carlisle brought with him through time. Tom picked it up and flipped through its pages. Finding something, he stopped to study it.

"Rex," Tom's tone was serious, "look at this."

Rex, not quite seeing the big deal, confirmed, "It's a Bible."

"Yeah, but look at this note."

Tom opened up the Bible to the inside cover and read aloud the note that was scribbled onto it. "Given to Russell in honor of his high school graduation. Love, Mother and Father. June 23, 1863."

Rex stepped back, even more confused, "June 23, 1863?" He paused for moment, until the date finally registered, then looked at Tom, "Who *is* this guy?"

Tom didn't know but he was sure going to find out.

CHAPTER FOURTEEN

"A Man Who Knew"

Carlisle's meeting at one o'clock with Mitchell Bain came at the perfect time for him. He badly needed someone with the same spiritual perspective to communicate with. Mitchell was perceptive and listened with a kind and understanding ear. He could easily see Carlisle was bothered by what had just happened at the high school.

Carlisle was already in the middle of his story, "And I just simply mentioned the Bible. I meant nothing by it. The teacher informed me that she could lose her job over the matter."

Mitchell wasn't surprised, "Russell, this isn't the nation built on the Biblical principles set forth by our founding fathers. The Bible hasn't been taught in the public school system for many years, and prayer was taken out of school by a Supreme Court decision in 1962."

Carlisle's breath was stolen by his shock. *The government is a part of this, too?* Distraught, he couldn't help react, "Children not allowed to pray to the Lord in school? How unthinkable."

"It gets worse. We live in a society that, for all practical purposes, is devoid of Christ and His presence."

Carlisle hung his head, feeling his heart break for the Lord. Mitchell continued, "Most of the people who attend church live this way. They honor Christ with their lips, but their hearts and service are far away. Because of this, many others have been turned away by these professing 'believers', which greatly hinders the spreading of the gospel. It's a wonder anyone comes to Christ these days."

Bargain night came to Carlisle's mind. He absolutely had to share this shocking experience with his new friend. "Last evening," Carlisle began, "I attended a 'movie' with a group from the church. The person on the screen blasphemed the name of our Lord!"

Russell Carlisle, unknowingly, had just unlocked the secrets of Mitchell Bain's past.

Before he became a Christian, Mitchell Bain worked for a major theater chain in a large metropolitan market as a booker and manager. He knew the movie industry well and the trappings that went along with it. He recognized the power of the media and the movies, especially movies, and their influence on millions of people...mostly for evil. Mitchell was a top executive, a shrewd businessman and appeared to be on top of the world. He was well off financially, had a faithful wife (though he had two affairs during this time) and three healthy children. He was not afraid to use unethical means in order to keep top clients happy. Many times, the larger studios would open big budget films in his area and they would flop. Mitchell would often "steal" box office money from the smaller independent films so he could give a better financial return to the larger studios. It was easy to justify. The big studios provided a consistent stream of movies featuring the major movie stars, which the theater needed to keep its doors open and stay profitable. The smaller independents were there one day and gone the next. Even with all of his success, though, Mitchell was unhappy, miserable and empty inside. There had to be more to life than making money and keeping ahead of the next cutthroat competitor.

One day, Mitchell met with an old high school buddy who had also done well, and had everything wealth and success could offer. He too though, had found himself feeling unhappy and miserable inside. He explained to Mitchell how he started to study the claims made by Jesus Christ. He came to understand why Jesus came to this earth to die for the sins of the world, and that Jesus wanted to give eternal life to anyone who followed Him as Lord and Savior. By receiving Christ by faith, his life had taken on new meaning and purpose. Mitchell was deeply touched by his friend's testimony and began to examine the Bible and its teachings. Shortly after, Mitchell humbled himself and committed his life to follow Christ. Life had not been the same since. He gladly left the movie industry, his unethical ways and extramarital affairs, and moved his family back to the city where he had been raised.

Mitchell Bain, the once proud, successful executive took a job as a librarian at the public library. The pay was not substantial, but honest work brought Mitchell peace of mind and many opportunities to share his newfound faith in Christ with others. He had been a librarian fifteen years now.

So, when Carlisle brought up the entertainment industry, he was talking to a man who knew.

Mitchell shook his head, "Russell, secular entertainment is probably the number one tool used by the Devil to deceive people and draw them away from the Lord."

"What do you mean?"

"The Devil has desensitized the entire world through what we call entertainment. Through the use of secular movies, videos, television and music, the Devil has blinded the eyes of man towards the things of the Lord, giving him a myriad of other distractions to occupy his time and thinking. Murder, violence, sexual immorality, greed, divorce, homosexuality, all of these sins have been subtly accepted by society so it's now second nature to all of us. We've seen all of these things so many times; it's no longer startling anymore. We, as a people, have lost our ability to discern, almost nothing shocks people."

"Why do people partake of these things?" Carlisle was trying to understand.

"Out of boredom, mainly. People are looking for things to do and as a result, will expose themselves to ungodly entertainment that totally opposes Christ and His teachings. The sad part is that most people, even many professing Christians, see nothing wrong with it and claim they are unaffected by it. The divorce rate in the church though is now the same as in the world and I blame it chiefly on our entertainment. Secular media is set up to make us dissatisfied with everything: our cars, our material possessions, our lifestyles, and even our mates."

"But..." Carlisle was still trying to comprehend, "Why were these things ever allowed?"

"For one thing, the Devil is smarter than most people give him credit for and very deceptive. Back in the 1930s, when movies first became popular, they were, for the most part, moralistic. There was a censor board that regulated what could be shown on the screen and moviemakers were very careful as to what they portrayed. However, what most people didn't realize is that Satan, at that point, had just won his greatest victory."

Carlisle was intrigued by the history lesson, "How so?"

"Because he eliminated *Jesus* from the movies. True, the moral and Biblical principles were still there, but not the Lord Himself. When you remove the Lord from the equation, you remove the Authority behind the teaching and, eventually, people become liberal in their views until there is little conviction at all. You wouldn't believe what one can see on that movie screen. Nudity, extreme acts of violence and, most disheartening, many movies blaspheme the name of the Lord."

Carlisle sat back dismayed at what he had just heard. *I was wrong. My own theory has just been proven wrong. Has my book contributed to the demise of this day?*

"I should have listened to Norris," Carlisle said aloud, to himself.

"What's that?" asked Mitchell.

Carlisle tried to cover up, "Oh I was just thinking about something Norris and I were discussing recently, something he was right about."

"Norris is a wise man."

"Yes, and a good friend. One who is not afraid to tell the truth."

"We all need friends that will be honest with us," Mitchell reaffirmed, remembering how his high school buddy had told him the truth about Christ so many years ago.

Carlisle was still dumbfounded by what he has just heard, "How could anyone in his or her right mind do anything that is such a mockery of the Lord? Do these moviemakers not know that the Lord God is the One who created them and gives them their every breath?"

Mitchell was almost glad Carlisle was upset by all of this. At least someone else saw the ungratefulness that abounded. He summed it all up, "Russell, the fear of the Lord is the beginning of wisdom. If a man does not fear the Lord, he will easily fall prey to the Devil. What else can be expected?"

CHAPTER FIFTEEN

"The Visitation"

Tuesday night was visitation night at the church, where church members visited the homes of people who had indicated an interest in hearing more about joining the church or perhaps desired to discuss spiritual matters. Carlisle had to attend. He had noticed so little effort in sharing the gospel in this modern age that he wanted to jump at every opportunity to influence others for the Lord. Everyone met at the church first, before splitting into small groups and taking different assignments. Carlisle, admittedly, hoped to see Ann there. He wanted to see how she was and wondered if she was still upset with him. He hoped he hadn't caused her too much trouble. Much to his disappointment, neither Ann nor Tom showed up. In fact, very few people showed up, eleven in all, including Carlisle. Considering the church had over seven hundred members, this was very disappointing, to say the least.

Carlisle feared he might be in the wrong place. He

stopped a man he recognized from his Sunday school class, the same the person who encouraged the class to attend the event.

"Pardon me," he asked politely, "is this where we meet for the visitations?"

"This is the place," the man assured him.

Carlisle double-checked, looking around at the lack of people, "Where is everybody?"

The man chuckled, "What do you mean, this is a pretty good turnout."

Carlisle was surprised, "Good turnout?"

The leader of the group spoke up, "Okay, let's get started, we have several names here." He started to hand a stack of visitation cards to someone nearby, "Could you please pass these around?"

Carlisle stood off to the side. Observing the scene, he recalled a Bible verse in Matthew chapter seven that had always scared him. *Narrow is the way that leads unto life and few there be that find it.* Yes, few. That was the scary part. Carlisle knew the Bible well and that it clearly stated only a few people would enter into Heaven because only a few people would humble themselves before the Lord and see their need for His saving grace. He had shared this many times with his students, although he wished the sad facts weren't true. However, he remained faithful to the Bible by teaching it. It broke Carlisle's heart at the same time, but now he believed it more than ever. He could see it before his own eyes. He only hoped the Lord would use tonight's effort by those who did attend in a mighty way.

****

Carlisle was placed with Doris and her husband, Bill, who were quite the pair. They were in their fifties and had a unique relationship. They argued constantly, over everything. Everything. Deep down, it was obvious that Bill and Doris deeply loved each other, it was just that their constant arguing made Carlisle wonder how they were ever married in the first place. He didn't know how to react to them, having never seen a man say the things Bill said to his wife. Carlisle was once again feeling alone and very out of place.

After some colorful banter between Bill and Doris over which house to visit first, they, along with Carlisle, were on their way. They pulled up to a modest home, parked, and made their way up the drive.

"Now let me do all the talking, Doris," Bill said sternly, "you ruined all our visits last week."

With a huff, Doris slapped Bill on the arm; "I did not."

Bill held up his visitation card for Carlisle to see, "It says on the card this family is really interested in joining the church. So, this one should be easy."

"Shall we pray first before we enter?" Carlisle seemed cautious.

Bill waved him off while ringing the doorbell, "No need to, we already prayed back at the church."

Carlisle frowned in disagreement as a lady prospect opened the door. Bill and Doris, all smiles, entered, while Carlisle stayed back for a second, perplexed.

****

The visitation was in full swing. Bill, Doris, Carlisle, the lady prospect, and her husband, were all sitting together in the family room while their two children, twelve and ten, were watching the television nearby in the next room with wide eyes and uncompromising interest. The television set, serving as the blazingly loud backdrop to the visit, was almost drowning out the conversation at hand.

Taking the lead, with Doris at his side, Bill was doing all the talking, speaking with the lady prospect and her husband. Already in mid-conversation, Bill was pitching hard, "And we have church volleyball teams, basketball, and softball. Some of the guys want to start a church golf league in the summer."

"Oh, Jerry, you'd love that," the lady said turning to her husband with an encouraging smile.

"You a golfer, Jerry?" Bill was making small talk, trying to win them over.

"Every once in awhile," Jerry responded, less than enthusiastic.

Bill noticed the kids watching television in the other room. He could use that. "We also have great programs for the kids. Twice a year we have big trips like going to Six Flags and major league ballgames."

The noisy television had become annoying by now. The lady prospect turned to her kids in the living room and called out politely, "Kids, please turn that down."

Neither child responded, but this got Carlisle's attention focused on the television.

Bill continued on, "Two years ago, the high school group went to Disney World and -"

The lady prospect noticed that neither child moved to turn the TV down and was now fed up. She swung her head back and this time impatiently shouted at her kids.

"HEY! I said turn the television down, *NOW!*" Then, with a complete change of attitude, turned to Bill with a polite smile, "Sorry."

Carlisle was perplexed at the woman's behavior, and at the children's. One of them finally got up enough energy to press the remote turning down the television volume...a little. Seeing that his assistance wasn't really needed at this particular moment in the visitation, Carlisle quietly left his seat and moved into the room where the children were watching television. Their eyes were glued to the screen.

Carlisle tried to start a conversation, "Hello, children."

The kids didn't even look up. Nothing was going to separate them from their show.

"Hey," said the older child, not looking away from the TV.

Carlisle decided to see what was so fascinating on the television and began to watch it. On the screen, he could see a couple was starting to move closer to each other, as if preparing for an intimate and passionate kiss. As Carlisle saw this, he began to feel uncomfortable and antsy.

"Oh..." his face was becoming flush, "Oh my."

The couple began to kiss and immediately Carlisle threw himself between the "innocent" children and the television screen.

"Oh my, my, my. What is this couple doing?" Carlisle questioned, appalled.

The kids were confused and annoyed.

"HEY!" the boy whined. "What are you doing, mister?"

Beside himself, Carlisle shook his head saying, "I cannot fathom this married couple would kiss in front of children! What is becoming of them?"

"What do you mean 'married couple'?" The girl asked.

"This married couple, *here*!" Carlisle restated pointing to the TV. "The ones that were just kissing in front of us."

"They're not married," the girl said, rolling her eyes.

Carlisle gasped, "Not married? I do not understand."

"They're just actors in a show," said the girl to straighten Carlisle out.

The older boy was fed up, "Come on, mister! Get out of the way!"

Bill, seeing the disturbance in the television room, peeked his head over the couch and called out, "Everything all right, Carlisle?"

Carlisle had no clue as to what was going on. In disbelief, he muttered to himself, "Not married?"

CHAPTER SIXTEEN

"Secret's Out"

When Tom Sharp walked into his office on Wednesday morning, Russell Carlisle was on his mind. Carlisle was a man with a secret, a huge secret, Tom knew that much for certain. He should because Tom knew a lot about secrets; he kept them every day. From his wife. From the IRS. It was thanks to secrets that Tom Sharp had acquired the things he had in this life. A beautiful home, a prosperous business and enough cash to last a lifetime. It was also these secrets, though, that made him vulnerable. If the right people, that is to say, the *wrong* people, found out about the things Tom did "off the records," he could lose everything. Paranoia, greed and guilt led to Tom's closed off attitude. He had become cold, cunning and an aggressor. He was the type of person who was going to get enough dirt on you before you could get any on him. Blackmail wasn't beneath Tom; it was just a tool to be used.

Tom had something on anyone he felt could threaten him and his security. He didn't go around talking about it to others, though. He just kept it to himself, on reserve. If anyone ever caught on to what he was doing after business hours, he was prepared to make that person an offer. An exchange of information. Nobody was going to get one over on him. Nobody. Not even his best friend, Rex. Tom had a file on Rex too, just in case. Rex didn't know it though, and Tom wasn't about to share it. He just kept it quiet. If information was power, Tom was a power broker. Now, this power broker was on to Carlisle. It provided a diversion from routine. Tom had a different chase to break up the monotony of his normal dishonest activities.

At his desk, Tom was on-line checking late morning stock quotes on his computer. The phone rang.

"Tom Sharp," Tom's greeting was quick and to the point.

"Me, again." It was Rex's voice.

"Find out anything?" Tom asked.

"Not much," Rex said disappointed. "He had a pretty normal morning. Went out to eat, then in and out of a bunch of shops for the rest of the time." Rex paused, as if forming a puzzled expression on the other end. "The guy acted as if he'd never seen any of this stuff before. Really took a lot of time looking at the simplest things. I can't figure out what he's up to."

Tom was confused too. "Did he buy anything?"

"Just something from a Christian bookstore. A book, I think. I didn't get a good look at it."

Tom confirmed their plan, "I set it up with Pastor Bergin. Carlisle's going to be sharing a few words during the service tonight."

"Good, that should give us some insight as to what he's up to."

Rex sounded confident because he had seen Tom use the church before. Those hallowed halls were good for confessions. Moved by the spirit, guilty parties were quick to confess their faults. It made Tom's hobby a lot easier. No digging involved. Just show up and watch those nasty little secrets come out.

"I think it's time we had a few words of our own with Mr. Carlisle before the service," Tom added getting into this interrogation game.

"Try to rattle him a little?" Rex said, playing along.

"Why not?" Tom replied, proud of himself. "He can't keep this 'top secret' act up forever."

"Yeah," Rex laughed in agreement. "See you tonight."

Tom listened to Rex hang up on the other end. Tom did likewise and rested the receiver back in its cradle.

"Tonight," Tom said softly, the word forming on his lips. One way or the other, Tom knew he would get to the bottom of this matter tonight.

****

Carlisle was anxious to get over to the library by one o'clock to once again visit his friend Mitchell Bain; he had several questions to ask him. Plus, he thought it proper to give formal farewells to his new confidant, encouraging him to keep the faith and continue being a beacon of light in this dark age. As he arrived at the library and entered, the secretary quickly dashed his plans.

"Oh, I'm sorry, sir," she replied when Carlisle asked to speak to Mitchell. "Mr. Bain had to go unexpectedly to the state office this morning. He won't be back until Friday."

Carlisle frowned, "Oh, I see."

The secretary eyed him, curiously, as if trying to place his face. "You're Mr. Carlisle, right?"

"Yes, I am."

She smiled, "He wanted me to tell you that–" she reached behind the counter, pulling out a sticky note, and began to quote it, "–he 'enjoyed meeting you, please give my best to Norris, and have a safe journey.'"

"Then," she interjected with humorous undertones, "he has in little bracket thingies, 'wherever that may be.'" She sat the note down and looked up to Carlisle, "He said you would understand."

Carlisle smiled, appreciative Mitchell was so courteous to leave a note in his absence. He bowed, like a gentleman, and replied, "Please give Mr. Bain my kindest regards. I enjoyed meeting and speaking with him, more than my words can convey." He thought about his message for a moment and then added, "Would you inform him that it was very educational?" Then, with a twinkle in his eye, Carlisle tried to mirror Mitchell's sentiment. "He will know what *I* mean."

The secretary smiled amused at Carlisle's reply. "I'll tell him," she chuckled.

Carlisle tipped his hat to her and began to leave as she went back to work. However, something caught his eye. Across the way, in the "kiddie corner" of the library, a microfiche computer pulled at him with its attention grabbing advertisement. On a poster board, scribbled with bright colors, as to attract children, the sign read:

TRAVEL BACK THROUGH TIME AND LEARN
ABOUT THE PAST!

Carlisle jumped out of his skin. *Remarkable! Could*

this be a portable time machine? He quickly returned to the counter and addressed the secretary.

"Pardon me," his excitement could hardly be contained.

The secretary looked up and smiled once again when she saw it was Carlisle. He smiled back, a little sheepish he bothered her again, "I was wondering..." as he pointed over to the microfiche, "What is that?"

The secretary peeked above the counter and spotted the computer. "That's a microfiche. It's a computer that let's you look up old newspaper articles in a town's history. It's a great way for the kids to discover the past," she finished, giving away the true purpose of the machine.

Carlisle had no problem with educating the children, "Certainly," he agreed. Then, he couldn't help ask, "Would it be too much to ask if someone could assist me, perhaps, in its usage?"

The secretary nodded her head, trying to relieve Carlisle's tension, "No, not at all. I'll get Greg to help you."

****

Moments later, Carlisle found himself sitting at the microfiche time machine. Greg, the resident helper, stood over his shoulder, pointing out the various features on this wonderful machine. Greg was already in mid-explanation, "Okay, here you go, Grace Bible Seminary. Is this what you want?"

Carlisle watched all of the bright colors and features on the computer. Everything was so fascinating. So fascinating, in fact, he could barely reply, "Yes. Yes, it is."

Carlisle squinted, trying to get a better look so he

could fully enjoy the microfiche experience, "This print is very small and difficult—"

Greg didn't give him time to finish. With the click of a button, the program zoomed in, expanding the print size to a readable format.

"Much better," Carlisle stated. "Thank you."

Carlisle's attention returned to the screen as he began to read. He still squinted though, blinded by the phosphorus screen. His 1890 crafted eyeballs weren't accustomed to the retina torture of the future and computer screens. Greg slowly scrolled information on the screen when Carlisle's eyes caught something familiar to him.

"Wait!" He shouted, excited that he recognized something, "Dr. Norris Anderson! I know him!"

Greg shot him a quizzical look, "What do you mean 'you know him'? The guy's probably been dead for over ninety years."

That grim realization sank into Carlisle's soul. *Of course. Norris would be dead.* This was over a hundred years in their future, but still, it made Carlisle homesick. He wanted to see his friend, alive and well in the nineteenth century. Saddened, he recovered, "I…I mean, I know *of* him. A brilliant Bible scholar he is…was."

Carlisle sat quietly for a moment before Greg leaned in to point out one more thing, "You can search for names and subjects by just typing in the key words right here."

Greg demonstrated.

"I see," Carlisle replied. "I think I might have it now. Thank you for your assistance."

"All right," Greg nodded as he got up, preparing to leave, "if you need any more help, just ask. I'll be around."

As he left, Carlisle called out behind him, "Thank you again."

Greg was gone and Carlisle was left alone to fend for himself in the wonderful world of microfiche. But, what should he ask the computer? Where, in time, did he want to go? He could track down some of the things Mitchell had talked about: the invention of the "movie;" the Supreme Court ruling to exorcise prayer from school; or find out what went wrong with the church. He had the entire history of modern day civilization at his fingertips. The only question he had to answer was where he wanted to go first. He thought about it, long and hard. Then, with a devilish grin, he got an idea. He looked around first, as if feeling guilty, and made sure no one was watching. He typed in a name.

R-U-S-S-E-L-L- C-A-R-L-I-S-L-E.

The computer began to process the information asking Carlisle to wait for a moment. Carlisle anxiously stared at the screen. While waiting, he started to get dizzy. The whole room began to swim around him and he could barely see. He had a terrible feeling inside. Then, he heard the words of Norris loud and clear in his mind as if Norris were standing right next to him.

"And do not try to look up your own fate, for it will not be revealed to you."

Feeling sick and struggling, Carlisle reached over and turned off the computer. Immediately, the dizziness went away and his vision immediately cleared up.

He would never know his fate.

****

Wednesday night church service was a sanctuary for some and a burden for others. To the ones who longed to fellowship with believers behind the safe doors of the Lord's house, Wednesday night church service was a welcome event. However, very few of *those* people attended this church. The rest came through the church doors out of obligation.

Carlisle was happy to be out of the library and to have escaped the attention of anyone who might have possibly seen his dizzy spell. Norris had warned him, like he did so many times before, but Carlisle didn't listen. So, as he arrived at the church, he was ready to live his last night in the future.

He entered tonight's service with a sense of nervousness. Out of the blue, earlier in the day, Pastor Bergin called Carlisle at the hotel and asked him to share a few words with the congregation. *Most splendid,* Carlisle first thought. He had learned so much in these last few days. Of course, now as Carlisle passed through the double doors, his anxiety was getting the better of him. *What should I say? Why me?* These people were born and raised in this time period. He had only been here for a little over four days. This might not be so splendid after all. This was not like lecturing his students, back at Grace Bible Seminary. He was out of his element, here. A stranger. An outsider. In this case, he felt as if *he* were the student. Then again, this was an opportunity. Carlisle just had to put his trust and faith in his Creator and Father.

Carlisle, keeping his butterflies in check, moved down the corridor towards the sanctuary. As he neared its entrance, he passed an intersection to another hallway and right past Tom and Rex. They had been waiting for him and were ready for business.

"Mr. Carlisle," Tom called out, "mind if we have a word with you?"

Carlisle stopped dead in his tracks and turned around. "No," he said with a nervous smile, as he walked towards the two.

"Oh, wait. It's 'Dr. Carlisle', isn't it?" Tom quickly continued. "What is it exactly, are you a doctor *of*? Where did you go to school? We have many contacts with the colleges. Maybe we know some of your teachers or classmates."

Carlisle held his ground. Tom's questions weren't really questions. Carlisle knew that. They were intimidation tactics. Carlisle knew that, too.

"What can I do for you gentlemen?"

Tom smiled like a jackal. He had nothing illegal on Carlisle. Just some unanswered questions and a few clues that didn't add up to enough change for a soda. So, he did what any bully would do in this situation, he bluffed. "We know what's going on with you Carlisle. We know all about the experiment."

Sweat formed on Carlisle's brow. *My secret is out,* he panicked. He felt hot and scared. "You do?" Carlisle said trying to remain cool. "H...how...who told you?"

Tom's grin was wide. *Gotcha.* He looked towards Rex who pulled something out of his back pocket. A police badge.

Carlisle was confused. Tom felt the need to clear it up. "Rex does all the background checks for the city police."

"And, I did some checking up on *you*," Rex added.

Carlisle felt betrayed. *They have been spying on me.*

"What do you gentlemen have against me?" Carlisle said pleading his innocence. "I have not harmed anyone, and I do not believe you truly know why I am here."

"Maybe you can enlighten us," Rex smiled, almost friendly. Proud of the fact he and Tom had Carlisle cornered. It felt good to be in the know and to have the upper hand.

Carlisle, however, had the true upper hand. After his

panic began to subside, he realized there was no possibility these men knew who he was. The only ones to even *know* about the time travel experiment were he, Norris, and the late John Anderson. They were only bullying him, and whether by their own device, or a much more sinister and unseen force, they were keeping him from sharing what the Lord had laid on his heart. Fear of public speaking or no, Carlisle wasn't going to stand for that. Boldly, he took two steps closer and stood his ground against Rex's smug smile.

"I'm afraid, detective," Carlisle spoke sternly without abandoning his gentlemen nature, "even if I told you, you would never believe me."

Tom was getting angry. Frustrated. "Why don't you just tell us the big secret, Carlisle?"

Carlisle stuck to his guns, always keeping in mind those church doors and his destiny on the other side, "I am not at liberty to disclose my purpose for being here, but I assure you it is completely innocent and perfectly legal."

Tom leaned in closer, taking one last crack at his intimidation tactics. His voice was low and full of harmful intent. "We're going to find out what's going on, you know that don't you, Carlisle?"

The scary thing was, Carlisle *did* know that.

"If you gentlemen will excuse me," Carlisle said with a smile and headed for the doors.

Rex turned to Tom, wide eyed, not knowing what to do next. He felt the control of the situation slipping out of their grasp. Tom came to the rescue as he called out, "Hey, Carlisle. Does the date June 23, 1863 mean anything to you?"

Carlisle froze. Tom wasn't sure what button he would hit, but seeing Carlisle's reaction brought his smile back.

He stood taller and folded his arms. *That did it,* he thought.

Carlisle's mind worked quickly wondering what he could say in his defense? What satisfactory explanation he could offer? *They must have seen my Bible. What will be enough for these people to leave me alone?* Then, he realized there would never be *enough.* Not for these two. Some people were just born to persecute and Carlisle had no time for such types. He had work to do. The Lord's work.

He did not reply. Then, he sucked up his fear and his preconceptions and marched through the doors into the sanctuary and his destiny on the other side.

CHAPTER SEVENTEEN

"A Word to the Future"

The congregation was already in the middle of a hymn. Carlisle felt odd and out of place as he walked to the front of the pews. Avoiding the odd glances of the church, he made it to the front row and took a hymnal. He didn't quite know where the congregation was singing in the hymnal, but he recognized the song and joined in. He sang with all of his heart, feeling the sweet praises of God soothing his anxious spirit.

Behind Carlisle, avoiding his notice, Tom and Rex came through the doors and took seats near the back. From where he was positioned though, Tom could keep an eye on Carlisle. This was going to be good. Tom got a morbid satisfaction from the thought of Carlisle standing in front of a room full of strangers, trying to find the right words to say.

The song ended and the choir director motioned for the congregation to take their seats. As they did, Pastor Bergin took his customary place behind the pulpit. With a warm, if not well rehearsed smile, the Pastor began his introductions. "I want to thank all of you for coming to our Wednesday night service. It's great to see your faces tonight."

A few people responded to the Pastor's words in what was more of an informal setting when compared to a Sunday morning worship time. Tonight's service was more of a business meeting than a regular service anyway.

"We will be voting on some important decisions regarding our building program tonight," Pastor Bergin continued, "and I am glad you will be part of this important time for our church family. But before we do so, I want to first introduce a special visitor who is with us this evening."

Tom smiled. *Here we go.*

This announcement got the congregation's attention. They began to glance around the congregation looking for anyone out of place. After a few seconds, most eyes settled on Russell Carlisle. This was one night Carlisle did not like being the center of attention. He was a long way from home, from the committee of professors. With an encouraging smile, the Pastor held out his hand towards the guest in question.

"Dr. Russell Carlisle," he beckoned.

On cue, Carlisle commanded his knees to stop shaking and stood up. All curious eyes were glued to him. He could feel his face turning red and his fear of speaking in front of large crowds coming back to him. Maybe he could just say something quick and leave. Maybe he could just leave. It wasn't like he had to face these people. In a couple hours, he was scheduled to catch the next cosmic string to the century long past. The thought of this escape eased his nerves. On his way to the podium, Carlisle happened to glance towards the back pews and saw Tom and Rex, arms folded and grinning. With a new determination, and a true sense of purpose, he forced his numbing legs onward.

The Pastor continued his introduction. "Dr. Carlisle is a seminary professor visiting from afar. I have asked him to share a few words with us tonight. Afterward, we will continue with our business at hand. Would you please welcome Dr. Russell Carlisle."

With that, Carlisle was by the Pastor's side. After a pat on the shoulder like he'd known him for years, the Pastor took a pew leaving the floor to Carlisle, now alone in the spotlight. He smiled faintly. The congregation gave a polite, yet automatic, short round of applause for their guest. Tom and Rex applauded, too. Mocking him, they were. Carlisle could feel the sweat roll from his brow. In fact, that was about all he felt. His body was numb. Carlisle's tongue felt thick and heavy and he didn't remember what he was going to say. Now, he just stood up there. Speechless. Motionless. Everyone watching him. Expecting something profound. No. Not profound.

Entertaining.

Clearing his throat, a little louder than he intended, Carlisle prayed silently for the Lord's intervention and stepped out on faith. "Thank you, Pastor," he began. He turned and faced the congregation squarely for the first time. "I must admit, I was a bit surprised when Pastor Bergin asked me to speak this evening. I am not quite sure why I, in particular, was chosen for the occasion."

Tom's eyes lit up.

Carlisle continued, "But I will take this as an opportunity from our Lord to share some matters with you He has laid on my heart."

After these two sentences, Carlisle could sense the

mood of the room change. The lightheartedness was gone but Carlisle felt the Spirit of God's power coming over him.

"Friends," he began boldly, "I have been away for quite some time. In fact, a very long time. It would be most truthful to say that I have been living as if in another culture. A culture much simpler than the one I have observed here."

Carlisle's opening drew a few weary stares from some of the older ladies. He ignored them and continued, "This is not to say we have no problems where I have come from. Most assuredly we do. All people are born with the sinful nature and we have all gone astray from the Lord our God."

The Pastor, agreeing with Carlisle so far, muttered a friendly "*Amen*".

Carlisle wasn't finished, "However, let me say the things I have observed here these past few days have been, at the very least, startling. Frankly brethren, I have been shocked. In the third chapter of Paul's second letter to Timothy, the Apostle warns us about the last days. In verses one through five, Scripture says in the last days men will be selfish, proud, without natural affection, unthankful, unholy, lovers of pleasure more than lovers of God. The list goes on from there. From what I have observed, the state this society is now in, reminds me not only of the days of Noah just prior to entering the ark but also the days of Lot in Sodom and Gomorrah."

These statements raised several eyebrows from the congregation. Few cared for the direction this was going. These were good people, after all. At least, by *their* definition. Why was this Carlisle guy saying all of this to them and not to the heathens outside these walls and in the bars?

Carlisle knew he was preaching to the ones who needed it and continued, "In both instances, God sent devastating judgments upon the earth. Surely, my friends, these must now be the last days Paul referred to, and the Second Coming of our Lord Jesus Christ is imminent."

The congregation's collective face was blank. Some had already gone on to more entertaining things like drawing on the church bulletin or visiting with their neighbors, while the rest were staring at Carlisle with a dead expression. No "Amens" could be heard. No head nods. No acknowledgments this man could be speaking truth. Tom was smiling, enjoying the negative feedback.

Carlisle persisted, "Friends, we need to become a desperate people, telling others about the offer of eternal life that can only be found in receiving Jesus Christ as Lord. We must tell our families, our friends, yes even our enemies. We, who claim to know Christ and His truth, must tell others about the grace of God and the inevitable coming judgment. I observe sin today being more open and blatant than any other time in the history of our nation, and the church seems to have completely lost her power and influence in society."

Tom and Rex sat back taking notice of the crowd's growing anxiety. Many in the congregation were fidgeting now. Some had even joined in the unofficial church bulletin art contest. Others picked up a hymnal and started flipping pages, looking for anything to divert their attention. Carlisle took notice of the crowd's wandering minds. This wasn't going good, not good at all. Yet in a strange way, Carlisle was okay with that. He knew these people weren't rejecting him, they were rejecting God's Word. They were rejecting truth. Carlisle had truth on his side and that courage now overpowered any sense of fear he once felt. Carlisle could feel the words coming from him now, and he had no inhibition or thought of holding them back.

"Our guard is down and worldliness has crept into the church and taken control. Christ is no longer the authority in His own church. The humanistic thought of man has infiltrated this society and, for the most part, as much as it pains me to say so, the church too. Please do not misunderstand me, my friends–," one of the deacons *"harumphed"* at the mention of *"friends"*, "–I am not setting myself in a higher moral position than anyone present tonight. I too, have failed the Lord in many ways and am dependent on his cleansing blood. Yet, what has happened to the authority and power of Jesus Christ in His church and in the world that He created? It appears He has been exiled from our schools, governments, businesses, entertainment, our families, our entire lives. It appears He is honored with our lips but, in reality, our hearts are far from him. The Church should not be following the world, but leading it to the better life. This has become a Christless society!"

Carlisle stopped for a moment, searching the crowd. Looking for a sign of recognition. A sign he wasn't preaching to thin air. *Where are the people who are concerned for the things of God?* Carlisle felt as if he was scolding a group of children. His heart was on fire though and he couldn't keep this agony to himself anymore.

"Through your inventions of the radio, television, and computer, society is being bombarded with a plethora of distracting thoughts, conflicting ideas and alternatives. Thus, Jesus Christ, what He stands for, what He did for us, and who He is... has been all but lost! Jesus should have preeminence in the life of people who calls themselves born again believers. Surely, the Lord is right when He says few people will enter through the narrow gate to Heaven."

Carlisle looked out upon the faces of the congregation again and his heart ached. He saw that these weren't "bad" people, at least as the world defined bad. They weren't murderers or adulterers in the literal sense. In fact, as far as the world viewed them, they were good, decent, upstanding people. Most obeyed the laws of the land. Kept out of trouble. Helped out their neighbor when they could. These were moral people...*in their own eyes!!* That's when it hit Carlisle. Morals *only.* People trying to live a good life to merit Heaven instead of receiving the Son of God and believing what He did for them on the cross to gain salvation. *Do these people not realize that in God's eyes we are all murders and adulterers if we have hated and lusted in our hearts? We are all sinners separated from God needing a Savior? Do they not know we cannot earn our way into Heaven?* Carlisle could not be angry with these people. If anything, he felt sorry for them. He knew their "religion" was something taught to them by their parents, and to *their parents* by their parents' parents. This was tradition. A tradition, Carlisle felt, was in some small part his own fault as a result of his book. A world based on Biblical morals. *I believe we can use morals to attract people to Jesus.* His own words haunted him, now. How could he have been so blind? *Norris was right,* Carlisle mourned inwardly, *it will be deadly!*

"Friends," Carlisle began anew with a heavy heart, "I urge you this evening to reconsider your own relationship with God through Christ. Please be abundantly clear you have truly submitted yourself to Jesus Christ and have received Him into your life as your personal Lord. Jesus will not save any man he cannot command. If you have been pretending in your relationship with God, if you know in your heart you have never truly submitted to Him, I beg of you, do so tonight. Tonight is the night to call upon His Name. Now is the time to cry out for Christ to save your soul from the eternal hell and suffering that is to come. Judgment is coming. Just as God judged the world in the days of Noah and judged the cities of Sodom and Gomorrah, one final judgment is coming upon all of those who do not come under the cleansing blood of Christ for their sins. I am afraid, in the Church and world today, there are many who profess to know Christ, but their hearts are far away from Him and not saved."

Carlisle stepped back for a moment watching the people and their faces. He searched for some kind of reaction, some kind of change of heart in this congregation. These were the people of God, right? They should be saying *"Amens"* to these statements. However, as he looked upon the people, he saw no sign of change, no sign of hearts being softened to the call of the Holy Spirit. He could only see cold, dead hearts and bored people, put off by his sermon. Not willing to change, only willing to continue with their tradition. Carlisle frowned. He decided he had better bring this sorrowful occasion to a close.

"I apologize for speaking so soberly to you at this time," he continued, "but this is what is in my heart and I am much afraid it shall remain with me for a long, long time. Please remember this fact, we shall all live forever. We will either spend eternity in the presence of God or in that place of darkness where there shall be weeping and gnashing of teeth. A place the Bible calls the Lake of Fire. Please, please give your life to Jesus Christ right now. Your eternal dwelling place will depend on it."

This congregation was spiritually dead. Russell Carlisle might as well had walked into a bar and preached the gospel to a bunch of drunkards. At least, *they* might have realized their rebellion towards God that had separated them from their Creator. The shocked and self-righteous silence of the congregation forced Carlisle to take a step back. Humbly, he bowed his head and muttered, "I...I have said enough."

Carlisle moved away from the podium and started walking down the stairs to his seat. The Pastor pulled himself up from the pew and approached the pulpit, reclaiming it. "Well," the Pastor began, shakily, "thank you, Dr. Carlisle. I am sure we will all take what you have said to heart." Then, as if Carlisle had never even existed, the Pastor turned to his people and completely changed tracks, "All right, then, as the men prepare to pass out the voting materials, why don't we all stand together and sing 'Amazing Grace'?"

The congregation stood to their feet, cracking open their hymnals, and began singing as if they loved the Lord with all of their hearts. Carlisle stood back and watched. He watched them change before his eyes from uncaring cold bodies to happy, cheery people. Were these his brothers and sisters in Christ? He was sure some...a *few*, were. Only the Lord knew. Carlisle didn't even stay for the entire song. Gentlemanly, he took his hat and Bible and quietly left down a side aisle towards an exit. He looked back for a moment to study the congregation again. After a sigh that emerged from deep within his soul, he left.

Rex was singing with the biggest smile on his face, he had gotten what he came here for. Tom was not. He saw Carlisle leave and motioned to his friend. They followed him.

CHAPTER EIGHTEEN

"Eddie: Round Two"

Carlisle proceeded to his hotel unaware Tom and Rex were in tow. He quickly changed back into his 1890 apparel and gathered his two modern suits and hat along with a package. He took the remaining money from his pocket, about sixty dollars and some change, and laid it on the dresser. He had no use for this money now and knew someone else would benefit from finding it. Before leaving, Carlisle took one last look out his room window where he had studied life on the streets each of the previous nights. He was very defeated; wishing he could have done more to help but realized the task was way too big for any one man. He had to trust in the sovereignty of God to accomplish His purposes.

As he left the hotel for the last time, he began walking towards the alley, still unaware of Tom and Rex's presence. First, Carlisle stopped for one final visit with a special friend. A friend he had grown to love and had been praying for every night since he met him. Eddie Martinez. The Laundromat was on route to his departure point and Carlisle still had some time. There was only one customer in the Laundromat when Carlisle entered. Still, Eddie did not see Carlisle approach him.

"I am leaving now, Eddie," Carlisle said with a determined finality in his voice. Eddie, already in the process of working on some undisclosed project underneath the counter, looked up to see Carlisle packed and ready to leave.

"Hey okay, Preacher," Eddie sounded confused but wasn't ready to argue the point, "take care."

"I have a couple of things I would like you to have." Carlisle reached under his arm and draped his fine new suits over the counter and before Eddie. "I have no use for these fine suits anymore," Carlisle explained.

Eddie smiled at the sentiment but couldn't fight the urge to tease his newfound friend, "I think these might be too small for me, Preacher."

Carlisle smiled, appreciating the humor. However, his smile fell short. A great sadness found its way into Carlisle's heart. He realized this was the last time he would ever see Eddie again. Carlisle explained the suits' purpose further, "I was hoping you could find someone who would benefit from their use."

Eddie smiled, "Yeah, Eddie will find somebody."

"And," Carlisle paused, trying to find the right words, "I want to leave this with you."

Carlisle pulled out a Bible. This was the book that Rex saw Carlisle purchase at a Christian bookstore. Eddie was genuinely surprised, "Hey, a Bible, huh?"

"Yes."

Eddie took the Bible and began to thumb through it,

"Eh, it's in Spanish, too?" He smiled again, touched, "That's all right, Preacher."

Carlisle felt warmhearted. He was delighted Eddie liked the gift. However, simple pleasantries were not enough. Time was drawing short. Carlisle's message was urgent. He leaned in closer to his friend, not wanting to threaten, but wanting to make his point clear, "Promise me you'll read it, Eddie."

Eddie, not knowing what the future would hold, in fact, not caring, shrugged his shoulders and replied, casually, "I'll read it." His mind already wandering, Eddie turned over the Bible to see the cover, "Hey, it's even got my name on it."

Carlisle tried to break through the trance, "Promise me."

Eddie looked up at Carlisle, realizing Carlisle was taking this very serious.

"If Eddie Martinez says he'll read it, he'll read it," he defended.

Nodding his head, Carlisle accepted his words and backed down, "I believe you, Eddie. May the Lord speak to you."

Eddie continued to look over the Bible, mumbling his fascination of it in Spanish. He was very flattered to have received this gift, even if it was a Bible. Not many people had ever done much for Eddie Martinez. He was the kind of guy who had to sweat blood for everything he got. When a gift did come his way, there was always a favor attached. It was a hard lesson Eddie learned at a young age, especially growing up on these city streets. Nothing was for free. Carlisle was different from anyone Eddie had ever met. He was sincere and honest. Eddie liked him. More so, he respected him. To be given a gift, knowing that no strings were attached, was a great thing for Eddie.

Carlisle brought out his pocket watch, checking the time, which was, literally, running out before his eyes. He frowned. If only he had more time. Sighing, he said good-bye to his friend, "I must be on my way now, Eddie."

Eddie looked Carlisle in the eye and they exchanged a moment. Eddie did not realize he would never see Carlisle again.

"Hey, so long, Preacher. Take care, okay?"

Carlisle nodded. He began to walk for the door, then stopped for a moment. *This may be it,* he realized. What if Eddie never gets around to reading the Bible? This may be his last chance to hear the gospel before it's too late. Carlisle couldn't take that chance.

He turned back to his friend, one last time, "Eddie, Jesus is coming back soon to set up his earthly Kingdom. The requirement to enter God's Kingdom is that we must be perfect and without any sin. But, no one is perfect, Eddie, we have all sinned. This is why we need to receive Jesus Christ into our life as Lord. He is the only person who has lived a perfect life and was therefore the perfect sacrifice on the cross for our sins. He rose from the dead, proving He is God, and wants to save us from the penalty of our sins and give us eternal life." Carlisle pointed to the Bible. "It is all in there, Eddie."

"I'm going to read this book, Preacher. I make you a promise and Eddie Martinez never goes back on his promise."

Carlisle could see that Eddie meant well. However, Carlisle knew what it meant to "mean well". It was not enough to have good intentions. A person needs discipline and commitment. Eddie smiled, trying to reassure Carlisle, but Carlisle's heart was heavy. He couldn't stress enough how urgent this matter was, "Please consider what I am saying," Carlisle reinforced.

With that, a sober Carlisle left the Laundromat, never to return.

****

Tom and Rex had watched the entire meeting with Eddie and started thinking that the two were in on something. They decided to follow Carlisle and would deal with Eddie later. However, this time, when Carlisle left the Laundromat, he saw both of them out of the corner of his eye. He glanced back towards Eddie for a moment, then began walking towards the ally pretending he was unaware he was being shadowed.

As Carlisle walked away from the Laundromat, Hector, Eddie's friend, entered. Hector was an older man, in his sixties, who also had his share of hard knocks in life. Eddie was still flipping through the pages of his new Bible, reading bits and pieces of it, when Hector called out to him, interrupting, "Hey, Eduardo!"

Eddie looked up and smiled when he saw his friend, "Hey, man, whatchoo doin?"

"How about a quick game of pool?"

Eddie laughed, "No, Hector. You no competition."

Hector smiled, prepared to defend his honor, "It won't take me but a minute to beat you."

"Hey, what you talking about?" Eddie continued to joke with him, "You can't beat me man."

Eddie leaned his head towards the back and called out in Spanish, "Hey, Margarita! Come up here!"

As Eddie called for his wife, Hector noticed the Bible. "What's this, man?" He asked.

Eddie smiled, remembering his friend Carlisle, "The preacher man gave this to me, it's a Spanish Bible."

Hector frowned and shook his head, "The preacher? You mean that guy you were telling me about?"

"Yeah," Eddie glanced out of the window trying to catch a glimpse of Carlisle who had already disappeared into the night, "he was different, that preacher."

"Eddie, that preacher is no good. He just wants your money."

Eddie was offended, "Why you gotta say that, Hector? That preacher was okay."

Hector tried to beat some sense into his partner, "Eddie, you don't need this." Hector took the Bible from the front desk and out of Eddie's grasp.

"Hey," he protested, "I promised the preacher I'd read it."

"Eddie, man," Hector sighed, "I'm telling you. Don't waste your time reading this stuff. You wanna become one of those religious nut jobs? You know how we hate those guys."

Eddie still felt the need to defend his friend, "Yeah? What makes you the expert?"

Hector waved the Bible in his hand, "I read this before and Hector knows a few things."

Eddie wasn't quite convinced of Hector's Biblical expertise, "Yeah, but that preacher, Jesus seemed real to him, man. Very real."

"Preachers are a lot of talk."

Hector was beginning to get to Eddie, even though he tried to remind himself how different Carlisle was, "Not this preacher, man."

"Eddie," Hector persisted, "God's not going to punish guys like us. Let me ask you, you ever murder someone?"

Appalled at the accusation, Eddie defended, "Eddie Martinez never hurt no one."

"You ever cheat on your wife?"

"On Margarita?! No way!"

Hector shrugged his shoulders, "Then you're going to Heaven. So don't mess with your mind, amigo. There's a lot of crazy religions out there and they're all after your money."

Eddie's will was starting to break down. He started to fall victim to his friend's easier way of thinking.

"Eddie Martinez is a good guy," he tried to convince himself, "he hurts no one."

Hector smiled, thankful he was getting this religious stuff out of Eddie's head. "Now come on," his true intentions were revealed, "One quick game of nine ball. I'm feeling lucky."

Eddie called back to his wife again, "Hey, Margarita! I'm leaving with Hector." Then, with a smile and all thoughts of the Bible far from his mind, he turned to Hector, "You still owe me three dollars."

Hector laughed, "Here's my chance to win it back. Double or nothing."

Eddie jumped the counter and led the way out the door towards the pool hall. Hector smiled and lagged behind for a moment. He took the Bible from the desk and tossed it into a nearby trashcan.

CHAPTER NINETEEN

"One Last Opportunity"

With Tom and Rex tailing him, Carlisle began to quicken his steps as he walked towards the alley and his departure point. He was nervous and beginning to sweat, not wanting to disclose the secret of the time machine. Carlisle was familiar with these surroundings, having spent time during his afternoons wandering around the area. There was virtually no one else in sight in this abandoned part of the city on this cool evening. In an attempt to lose his predators, Carlisle proceeded to a point where there were a number of buildings stacked closely together containing many passageways. Tom and Rex, who had been following from afar, now realized Carlisle was aware of their presence and sensed he was trying to lose them. They decided to split up. Carlisle was dashing in and out between the buildings, watching carefully to see if he could spot either of his pursuers. He couldn't. He stopped for a moment to catch his breath and checked his pocket watch.

It was now ten minutes to nine. Carlisle was only a short distance from the alley but wanted to make sure he could maneuver into position without being seen.

Carlisle spotted Rex across the street from him moving in the other direction. He also saw a shadow in the distance in about the same area, which he believed to be Tom. Relieved and thinking this was his chance, Carlisle headed in the opposite way to the alley. As he arrived, he stopped for a moment to make sure the coast was clear. It was. Carlisle then made his way to the exact spot that had bore witness to his birth in this new time. He checked his pocket watch again; it was seven minutes to nine. He was ready, almost glad to leave. Things here were just too...disheartening. He took a moment to remember what had just transpired back at the church. He had poured his heart out to those people and wondered if anything he said would take root. *Only the Spirit of God can allow a person to see truth,* Carlisle thought to reassure himself. His thoughts turned to Eddie. *I pray Lord you will use your word in a mighty way in Eddie's life.* Carlisle checked his pocket watch again. Six minutes to nine. He couldn't wait to get home to see Helen. He had missed her so much in this strange place. Her beautiful face would be a most welcomed sight.

"Carlisle!" Tom's voice startled Carlisle out of his thoughts of Helen. On his heels, he spun around and saw Tom, with Rex standing beside him.

"Gentlemen," he panicked, "you must leave here, immediately. There is not much time!"

Tom smiled. The pressure was on. He started to walk forward, backing Carlisle up against the alley wall, "Much time for what?"

Carlisle remained steadfast, "I am afraid I am not

allowed to explain. However, you *must* leave this area at once!"

Tom leaned in closer, "You know, we've had enough of your secrets, Carlisle."

"Yeah," Rex threatened in a bully-like manner, "I'm thinking about taking you downtown for some questioning unless you tell us what's going on."

Carlisle remained a gentleman. "I understand your concern. However, I have not hurt anyone, nor do I intend to. If I told you why I was here, you would not believe me. Now, if you please."

Tom was getting more determined, "We're not leaving, Carlisle."

Carlisle wanted to roar his frustration, "But there is not much time!"

Rex picked up on Carlisle's urgency. "You keep saying that. Much time for *what*?"

Carlisle checked the time. Two minutes to nine. He wished it would run faster to spare him another second with these two ruffians. *Hurry up, Norris.* Despite his desire to leave, Tom and Rex still stood before him, wanting answers. So, off the top of his head, he offered, "For Jesus...Jesus is coming."

Rex started laughing at the explanation, "Jesus is coming?"

Carlisle sensed he was on to something, "Yes, Jesus. I believe Jesus is coming..." he checked his pocket watch again. "Perhaps at any moment."

Rex started checking the skies. Tom raised an eyebrow, still suspicious. "Don't you think you're taking this a little too far, Carlisle?"

Carlisle rolled his eyes, "I told you, you would not believe me. So, if you please, just leave."

Rex was still amused with the Jesus story, but Tom was fed up. Tom angrily grabbed Carlisle's arm forcing him closer, "You're coming downtown with us."

Carlisle protested and jerked back. His demeanor now changed. He had put up with these two long enough. He had an idea. Maybe Tom and Rex, despite their lack of point, were here for a reason. Maybe God, in His infinite wisdom, had crossed their paths this night for a purpose. Maybe this was one last opportunity for Carlisle to get the gospel out in this generation before it was too late. So, ever the teacher, Carlisle took control and began the lesson.

"No, gentlemen, that will not be necessary," he said authoritatively. "You see, I am a messenger from the Lord and I have been sent to warn you Jesus is coming. Let me ask you. Do you know Him?"

Rex was eager to respond. Tom kept quiet and watched with disdain. "Of course we do," Rex replied without a thought.

"No," Carlisle specified, "not do you know *of* Him intellectually, but do you *know* Him personally? Do you have a living true relationship with the Lord Jesus Christ? Do you really see your need for Him?"

Tom wouldn't be pushed around, "Listen, Carlisle. We're church members. We don't need the sermon." His face was grim and intense. Carlisle's eyes met Tom's and they stared each other down.

"Yes, gentlemen," Carlisle spoke boldly and with power, "I believe you do. Like most people in the world."

Rex, still seeing it all as a joke, pleaded with Carlisle, "C'mon, Carlisle, don't make us use force. Let's just go downtown and talk for awhile, nice and easy."

Suddenly, the air began to blow around them. Loose trash was caught up and swirled upward. All three men could feel the hairs on the back of their necks standing on end. Carlisle checked his pocket watch.

Nine o'clock.

He smiled. *Right on time.*

For the benefit of Tom and Rex, Carlisle pointed to the skies. "LOOK!" He shouted as the wind picked up, so violently that his voice was hardly audible. "It's TIIIMM-MEE!!"

Just then, the heavens opened and the cosmic strings plummeted to the Earth. Carlisle was encircled in their bright yellow light, completely surrounded by their grasp. Then, in a brilliant show of light and wind, he vanished, as the cosmic strings retreated skyward.

After the fluttering trash settled back to a suitable resting place on the alley floor, Tom and Rex continued to gaze into the night sky. Their faces had turned white as they watched in awe and in disbelief, trembling in their shoes. Silence prevailed as the two men reflected on what had just transpired. In that moment, fearing the worst, they began to look inward to finally question their relationship with the Lord. Carlisle's work was now finished.

Rex turned to his friend, scared and stuttering, barely able to utter the words, "I think we just missed the Rapture."

CHAPTER TWENTY

"Time Changer"

Carlisle was instantaneously transported through time and space, as the cosmic strings returned him to Norris' shed. After deeming himself brave enough to open his eyes, he realized he was standing in the midst of the time machine. He made it! Everything was exactly as he left it. He was back home and almost to the point where he felt tears. Excitedly, he exited the platform and took a step back to look at everything. It had been five long days and he needed to re-familiarize himself with his world.

Then, behind the panel, taking off his safety goggles, Norris stepped into the moonlight. Carlisle saw his friend's sly smile and threw his arms up in the air, charging Norris, wrapping his arms around him. "Norris!" He exclaimed, "You are still here!"

Norris laughed. It had been a century since Carlisle last saw his friend, but to Norris, it had all been instantaneous. "Yes, my friend. You have only been away for a few moments."

Carlisle stepped back and looked at him with amazement.

"It is so marvelous to see you again!" Then, Carlisle turned to face the machine that had changed his life. He approached it with a newfound respect, not daring to mock it again. He patted the equipment.

"This machine is absolutely amazing," he whispered in awe.

Norris beamed, proud of the experiment and his father's dreams finally coming to pass, "Yes, the Lord has granted us a great privilege."

After sharing a moment with the strange contraption he had grown a bond with, Carlisle told his friend what he'd seen.

"Norris," he began soberly, "The future. Sin abounds! Christ is not feared. Morals have replaced Christ...and liberal teachings at that! Families are in total disarray, many not even families anymore. The world is essentially living without Jesus while the Church is full of professing Christians who do not know the Lord they claim they follow. I can almost see why the world is not listening to them. The Church has become lukewarm as the Lord forewarned in the Book of Revelation!"

Norris stood there, with a knowing concern, "Yes."

Carlisle took a deep breath, reliving the horror. Then, with sad conviction, laid a heavy hand on Norris' shoulder, "I am sorry I doubted you, old friend. You were right, Norris. I was wrong in my thinking, so very wrong. To separate the authority of Jesus from His teachings is, indeed, deadly. For..." he glanced back towards the machine, "I have just witnessed the product."

Norris joined his friend. "It will lead many astray."

Norris and Carlisle, their friendship now mended,

shared a moment of great sadness, mourning the generations that had yet to come. However, now Carlisle realized, perhaps he could do something about it. Maybe even prevent a small part of it from ever taking place.

"Well, I have a book to rework," he admitted.

Norris smiled, "I suppose you do."

Carlisle patted his friend's shoulder one last hearty time and began walking away. After a moment though, Carlisle stopped, but did not face his friend. His next question was too painful.

"Norris," he paused in thought for a moment, "did you ever see how far ahead the time machine would send someone into the future?"

Now it was Norris' turn to look over to the time machine. His expression, at first happy with Carlisle's change, slowly became grim.

"I sent you as far into the future as the machine would allow."

Carlisle hung his head. Quickly, in his mind, flashed images of some of the people he had met in the future. From Sunday School class, to Tuesday night visitation, Tom and Rex, their wives, the people at church, the eleven year old girl at the park and…Eddie. He knew they all needed Jesus or they would be doomed forever. He also knew their time was very short. So did Norris. Both of them, fearing what was to come. Then, silently, Carlisle left.

****

Monday afternoon of the next week, Dr. Norris Anderson found himself, once again, among his peers and colleagues in the meeting room at Grace Bible Seminary.

The usual committee members were there. All except one. Carlisle.

Everyone sat there, patiently awaiting their absent member. The Dean looked concerned. Norris couldn't hide his big grin. He knew what was keeping Carlisle.

Finally, a little out of breath, Carlisle came busting through the double doors. Under his arm, he carried a leather bound sachet. All of the members spun, at once, to face him. Once he caught his breath, he bowed to the Dean. "I apologize for my tardiness, gentlemen."

Wiseman spoke up, giving his friend a hard time, "Well, Dr. Carlisle, nice of you to attend. We were beginning to wonder."

The men laughed and Carlisle smiled, good-naturedly. The Dean watched him, stern and expectant. Carlisle again bowed to his superior, "My sincerest apologies, Dean."

The Dean nodded, accepting that. Carlisle took the bundle from underneath his arm and unraveled its leather straps to reveal his manuscript. His *new* manuscript. He proceeded to hand out individual copies to each member of the committee. As Norris' turn came up, the two friends exchanged a knowing smile.

Carlisle addressed his colleagues, "I am afraid, gentlemen, I am going to have to ask you to read through these necessary revisions before making your final decision. I shall be ready to reconvene at your first convenience."

Everyone looked confused.

"Is this a result of your meeting with Dr. Anderson?" the Dean asked.

Carlisle smiled at Norris first, then corrected the Dean, "This is a result of the Lord using one of his servants to open my eyes a little more to His glorious truth, sir."

The Dean gestured a job well done to Carlisle's reply,

"Very well then, Dr. Carlisle. We will review this new material and shall call another meeting."

Carlisle smiled and nodded back to the Dean, "Thank you, sir." He turned to his fellow professors, "And thank you, gentlemen." Carlisle bowed slightly, as was his way, and began to leave.

However, the Dean, after closely studying the manuscript, called out to Carlisle with curiosity, "Dr. Carlisle?"

Carlisle stopped and turned. The Dean continued, "I noticed you have changed the title of your book to 'Time Changer'."

Nodding, Carlisle confirmed, "Yes, sir. Times must change, or time, as we know it, will end."

Again, Carlisle looked at his friend Norris and smiled, humbly and sincerely. Leaving the Dean and the others behind to wonder about the change in him, Carlisle left.

****

Upon leaving the hallowed halls of Grace Bible Seminary, Carlisle was filled with unspeakable joy having never felt closer to the Lord or with more purpose in his life. He began walking along the pathway when he came across the same group of children he had caught singing near the building a few days before. This time, they weren't singing, just playing. When they saw Carlisle, they immediately became frightened, ceased their activities, and stood sullenly, eyes downcast.

Carlisle stopped for a moment, eyeing each youngster. His face was stern. They all looked worried. Then, with a compassionate look, his hard face cracked a smile and he began to sing the words to *"Oh How I Love Jesus,"* the same song Carlisle had scolded the children for singing earlier. Before giving the children any time to react, he held his hands behind his back and strolled along. All the children smiled and giggled, unable to contain their joy. They began singing the same rendition, as Carlisle walked away in the distance.

THE END

After the Credits

Recently, a friend of mine asked me if I was going to continue making films with a religious theme. His question caused me to consider the following. If you think about, in a sense, all movies are "religious". In fact, human beings, by their very nature, are "religious", too. Religion can simply be defined as having a set of moral standards and a belief in the supernatural. All people have standards and beliefs about morals and God. Our views may differ, but each of us has a standard which we live by. We do not yet live in a society where it seems right for people to indiscriminately kill one another. There is something within us (a God-given conscience), which tells us killing is wrong.

Movies, in turn, fall into the same category. Although called entertainment, movies present standards, morals and beliefs as well. Their views may differ and some standards are more liberal than others, but they all still adhere to a set of values. So, in truth, all movies are "religious" in nature, too. Whether it be a horror film, fantasy film, sci-fi film, no matter what the category, all films present moral standards, many times using a good versus evil theme.

The issue then is not whether something is religious; the issue is whether it is threatening. This is why it is so important to examine the claims of Jesus Christ. His message is life giving but, at the same time, also life threatening. The Bible clearly teaches each soul lives forever and will spend eternity in either heaven or hell. These are strong claims that threaten us and should demand our attention. I don't want to go to hell and if given the choice, would certainly choose the joy heaven promises. I do know for sure one day I am going to die and some type of afterlife awaits me. This fact threatens my security. I must be absolutely certain what I think and believe is based upon truth. I cannot choose what I want to believe and define that as truth but I must base my beliefs on absolute truth.

The ultimate goal in life is to gain heaven. The religions of man attempt to answer how to reach this destination. Heaven does exist, and I want to end up there. Don't you? We must do all that we can to make sure we are on the right track to get there. Most of the people living in this world, no matter what their faith, try to earn salvation or their heavenly reward. They reason if they just believe in God and try to live a good life they will go to heaven. Many believe that since God is a God of love He would never punish them. This is what I grew up believing. It sounded good, seemed right and was very convenient. However, was it correct? The Bible says there is a way that seems right to a man but the end results in (spiritual) death or separation from the Lord. (Proverbs 14:12) We better make sure this verse is not talking about us.

Though there are an endless number of religions in

this world, they essentially condense to only two. Either a person tries to earn salvation through doing good deeds OR they trust in the finished work of Jesus Christ for salvation, which only comes by receiving Him by faith as Lord. That's it. A world of religions, but only two kinds. Either you earn your own salvation or you receive it through Christ. Every human soul that ever lived falls into one of these two categories. It doesn't matter what religion you call yourself, you are in one of these two groups.

The Bible clearly teaches that a person cannot earn salvation. If one could, then why did Jesus have to die for our sins? We must understand the requirement to spend eternity in heaven is to be absolutely perfect or righteous as the Bible says. This is the standard we must meet. We know that no one is perfect though, and the Bible reaffirms this truth time and time again. The Scripture says all have sinned and fall short of the glory of God (Rom 3:23); there is none that does good, no not one (Rom. 3:10); there is none righteous, no not one (Rom. 3:12) and the unrighteous will NOT enter the Kingdom of God. (1 Cor 6:9) Since all of us have sinned, then all of us are unrighteous in God's eyes. These are strong statements that confront our soul with a major problem, which must be dealt with. These truths, like death, will never go away. Our sins have separated us from our Creator God. We must face these issues before it is too late because our eternal destiny depends on the choice we make.

This is where Jesus comes in and why we need Him. Jesus lived a perfect life. Jesus never sinned. Jesus was totally righteous. Jesus met the requirement. When we receive Jesus by faith as our personal Lord to follow Him, He cleanses us from our sins and makes us righteous in the sight of God...forever.

These are the answers that I struggled to find years ago in my early twenties when I became concerned about the real issues of life. Jesus Christ gives us eternal life in heaven and I am convinced He is the only way to get there. Jesus said it this way. "I am the way, the truth, and the life and no man cometh unto the Father but by Me." (John 14:6)

Recently, a friend of mine asked me if I was going to continue making films with a religious theme. My answer? I must continue making films that will provoke people to think about Jesus, their salvation and their eternal destination. We will all give account to God for what we did with His Son in this lifetime. I must promote Christ and His message. This is the most important issue in life. I hope you will take what is written to heart. Thank you for reading this and *Time Changer.*

−Rich Christiano

Coming...{if time doesn't end}

Time Changer 2

THE SEARCH
An Adventure of Reed Carlisle

FILMS BY RICH CHRISTIANO

End of the Harvest

A college philosophy club meeting filled with atheists humiliates a new believer as he tries to prove the existence of God. As a result, a Christian, out of fellowship with the Lord, seeks revenge. He comes across a paper written 50 years ago regarding a theory a student had about when the world might end. With this paper in hand, he sets up a showdown with the club for their next meeting. A compelling evangelistic drama.

Second Glance

High school senior Dan Burgess is a Christian but doesn't think he's impacting anyone for the Lord. He thinks he is missing out on all the fun and he is frustrated with his life. So one night, under his breath, he wishes he'd never became a Christian. Does he get his wish? A very inspirational film for teens and adults.

The Appointment

A newspaper woman is writing a series of anti-God editorials mocking God and making fun of the church. One day, she gets a visit in her office from a mysterious stranger who, claiming to be from the Lord, tells her that in eight days at 6:05PM she is going to die. Is this a hoax? Or the truth?

The suspense begins...

Available at
www.christianmovies.com
870-932-7018